SO-APP-328

The Deal
of the
Century

BY THE AUTHOR OF

Regan
The Manhattan File
The Deal of the Century

IAN KENNEDY MARTIN

The Deal of the Century

HOLT, RINEHART and WINSTON
New York

Copyright © 1976 by Ian Kennedy Martin

All rights reserved, including the right to reproduce
this book or portions thereof in any form.

Library of Congress Cataloging in Publication Data

Martin, Ian Kennedy.
The deal of the century.

I.   Title.
PZ4.M38116De3   [PR6063.A715]   823'.9'14   76-43497
ISBN: 0-03-089936-2

First published in the United States in 1977.
Designer: Kathy Peck

Printed in the United States of America

10 9 8 7 6 5 4 3 2 1

The Deal of the Century

Sheikh Hamid bin Haffasa cashed in his oil wells on Monday, the eighth of March, 1976, on the third floor of the Wellington Clinic, Lord's. The deus ex machina of this sudden demise was an M-38 submachine gun in the hands of a cool assassin. A whole clip of ammunition had taken off most of Haffasa's head and right shoulder and reworked the bed headboard and the floor and walls of the room in technicolor. The noise disturbed fourteen other millionaires who were losing their prostates in the privacy of one-hundred-pound-a-day suites. They all rang their bells simultaneously. It sounded like an Italian town on an Easter Sunday—not at all appropriate for a Muhammadan Croesus taking his final bows and heading for that last great gas station in the sky. . . .

1

Detective Inspector Jack Regan of the Flying Squad, New Scotland Yard, heard a noise like a muffled jackhammer being drowned out by the heavy truck traffic up Wellington Road. Afterwards he was to wonder why he hadn't identified it as gunfire. As a Metropolitan Criminal Investigation Department detective he had to check in every four months at the Lippets Hill police range and fire at least a hundred rounds during a whole day's gun practice. But he'd never heard the ultrafast bark of an M-38 before. And maybe the acoustics of the hospital had distorted the sound.

Regan was visiting the private suite of a West End villain named Harvey Cantwell, whom he'd known for some years. Cantwell had had a skiing accident, a broken leg which had been badly reset by a Swiss doctor. He'd been in the Wellington to sort that out. Cantwell's suite was at the north end of the long third-floor corridor. Sheikh Haffasa's suite had been down the other end of the corridor and around the corner, with a perfect view down over the felt-flat acres of the green turf of Lord's cricket ground.

For some days afterward Regan was to rethink over and over again exactly what he did from the time he heard the jackhammer sound, said his good-byes into the ill face of Harvey Cantwell, and walked from Cantwell's bedroom, through his living room, into the corridor, and down the corridor to the elevators.

At the elevators Regan met the murderer of Sheikh bin Haffasa. He was lighting a cigarette. He seemed relaxed, a man of medium height, neat, dark complexion, fortyish.

2

He'd left the M-38 with his fingerprints on it in the victim's room. He'd pressed the button for the lift and with a slight nod bowed Regan into it when it arrived. The cigarette the man lit must have been the last one in a Benson & Hedges packet. Regan noticed and remembered that the man dropped the empty packet onto the floor of the elevator. The fingerprints on the cigarette packet matched the fingerprints on the murder weapon. There was no record of the fingerprints in the Yard's files.

Regan rode from the third floor down to the ground with the killer. He remembered the man had gone out of the building and waved down a cab. That detail stuck in his mind as a measure of the murderer's cool. The neat-looking gentleman had entered the Wellington with the M-38, assassinated Haffasa, taken the elevator, lit a cigarette, and then wandered out into the street, apparently relying on the exigencies of the London taxi service for his getaway. The man who had butchered Haffasa had not calculated it would be necessary to make any particular arrangements for a speedy exit—like, for instance, a hired car.

He'd killed and then looked for a cab. That suggested to Regan that he was dealing with either an amazing professional or a maniac. And this was to concern him directly. Two hours after the coincidence of his being present at the Wellington Clinic, he was called in by the assistant commissioner of crime, Scotland Yard.

The ACC's message was curt. "Regan, DCI Mellin, St. John's Wood nick, is notionally in charge. But I'm allocating you to his murder squad on a roving commission.

Mellin's the boss, but as far as I'm concerned, you're the joker who's going to comb the country and locate this chummy."

"With respect, sir, I don't think this man's in the U.K. I think this is the kind of contract that's been fixed in Lebanon for some gun-crazy Cypriot or the like, to come into this country, in and out on a twenty-four-hour hit. And in my experience, sir, the motives for killing a black gold Arab this rich are never simple. . . ."

As it turned out, Regan was wrong in his first observation, and right in his second.

"The nose was thinner," Regan told the sergeant operating the photofit.

The sergeant looked in the little compartments of the kit to sort out a pile of nose varieties. He showed a sample to Regan.

"No," said Regan. "A thin nose, but the nostrils more flared. Imagine a white-skinned version of an adolescent Negro. You know, before he becomes all arms and the proboscis thickens up. . . ."

The young sergeant looked put out and started to skip through another half dozen nose profiles. Regan stood up and moved to the window of his office and looked out into the death of another London day, its dusk, the shadows sharpening as the neon offices switched off, the start of the commuter crawl out of the buildings in the shadows of Scotland Yard, the beginning of rain.

He could see all that, and he could also see his face superimposed, back-lit, on the windowpane. The reflection looked like a photofit picture, a sum of parts, not a cohesive whole. Regan was five feet ten, had thin hair that was curly and sandy, blue eyes filmed with red lines from an early start this morning after a sleepless night, two overnight bags under the eyes that would have done a Roman emperor proud, and a six o'clock shadow turning into stubble across the work surfaces of his face. He knew he looked a mess. He knew he was looking less and less like the leading detective in the "Sweeney"—the nickname for the Met CID's crack "Flying Squad." The leading detective because he had the track record, the highest statistics of arrests and convictions, to prove it. He was famous as a thief taker, infamous as a cavalier. The new-look Metropolitan Police of the seventies was run on the principles of committees, shared responsibilities and work loads. Inspector Jack Regan was a cop of the fifties, of the old school, of a personalized list of selected targets, of the virtuoso performance in thief taking. He ran against every grain in the woodwork of Scotland Yard. But he could get away with it, because he made it work. When a job file fell on the desk of the superintendent, Flying Squad, and it was a tough job, requiring perspicacity, wit, courage, and brilliance, the file went to Regan. But equally, someone in that establishment, or more than one because he had many enemies, would be collecting a list of his minor mistakes—he had not yet made a major one. Someone would be assembling a list, waiting for the day, the year, when he did make the first major mistake.

The night stretched before him void of plans. It was Monday and he had been duty officer last week, and somehow he'd forgotten to get something together for his evenings this week. For a month he'd been toying with a new girl, Sylvia, in Hammersmith, good-looking, with lots of past and no future. She lived just around the corner from his own digs off Chiswick High Road. Very convenient. He'd given her a couple and then had been bringing her along, coaxing her to relax and make him enjoy life a little. Underneath the horror show of her life—she was a mid-sixties hippie whose mother had killed herself—she seemed a reasonable kid and was *bon* in bed. But then last week she'd suddenly opened her mouth. She'd started to verbalize a skein of complaints on a variety of subjects, especially himself. "Why do all men only want one thing from me?" she kept asking Regan as he tried to sleep after he'd gotten it. It was a question which was puzzling him less about her. No, she'd have to go.

She'd delivered a philosophical diatribe last Friday at four in the morning. The subject was the history of the decline of Western civilization as seen through the collapse of the National Health Service, an event chaperoned into existence a month before when her local GP refused to prescribe any more Valium.

"Look," Regan had told her, "just think of life as mildly therapeutic. Don't get that worked up about it." But he had already made up his mind to exit.

So Monday had been for Regan, like the Arab sheikh in the Wellington, a lousy day. It was now 5:15 and he was waiting for the nervous photofit sergeant to get a face together, and waiting for a call from Special Branch, to be followed by a spectral evening, a six-pack of Watney's Pale to damp down a few more hours of depression, and TV, before a lonely bed. A healthy anger was boiling up in him. How the hell could the ACC not know that a killing like Haffasa's would not be made in Britain? No English-based artist would have relied on London taxicabs to get him from the crime scene. The killer hadn't even looked English.

The phone rang. The photofit sergeant answered it. "DI's office?" He and Regan were alone in Regan's office. "Oh, yes, sir." The sergeant turned to Regan. "Commander, Special Branch, sir."

Regan took the phone. "Evening, sir." He said the words gently—he knew the SB chief and liked him. "Look, sir, I was in on this charade at the Wellington Clinic this morning—all quite by accident. I actually accompanied the chummy who did the dirt down the lift to the ground floor. You heard?"

"Yes?" Commander Millward, head of England's so-called secret police, the Special Branch, replied. "What d'you want, Regan?" His voice was guarded, like he knew a request was in the offing.

"Look, sir, when I walked into the Wellington this morning I had plenty on my plate. I don't need this. I don't need to waste the next six months of my life chasing around London looking for a killer who lives in a bedsitter in Beirut or Bangkok."

"What are you asking, Regan?" Millward's voice was hardening.

Regan was not in the mood for diplomacy. "You want what I want. This is your lot, sir. This has got SB written all over it. I want you to phone the ACC. Tell him it's ninety-nine one-hundredth's that the Haffasa killing is an outside U.K. contract, politically motivated, and the fact that I saw some gook in a lift is neither here nor there . . ."

"Have we got an assassin's description—our SB lads?"

"Not yet, sir, I'm working on a photofit."

"A photofit I don't want. Have you got a police artist there?"

"We couldn't get our hands on an artist this afternoon."

"I'll get hold of one now. I'll get him immediately to you."

"Are you saying, sir, that you'll straighten the ACC?" Regan was unsure about what the SB chief was up to.

"Bugger off, Regan. You try a taste of it. We spend all our days chasing gooks, wogs, spicks, and spooks. You're the only man in the world who can positively identify the murderer. You also happen to be—the story goes, and you tell it more than anyone else—the best DI in the Yard. I see why the ACC put you on it. For our records I want a police artist's drawing of chummy. In future don't ask me to intercede between you and an ACC order. You should know better." Millward replaced the phone.

Regan, angry, replaced his, rubbed Millward's name off his mental list of Yard friends, and said, "Fuck." Not only was he stuck with a photofit sergeant who was going to take another two hours to sort out a face that would look nothing like the killer's, and a face that was already on a plane bound for the Galápagos Islands or points west, he was now going to have to spend hours with a bloody Yard artist.

He went to the hospitality cupboard, took out the keys, unlocked the door, reached in and took out the bottle of whiskey. It was 5:30 in the afternoon. The unwritten rule in the Yard is that no one opens a hospitality cupboard until around six. But Regan's depression was beyond rules. He was the top Flying Squad detective—his particular speciality the inner workings of the London criminal world. He didn't know anything about oil sheikhs, except that he didn't like them. He knew that his kind of feelings was not translated into action by any London criminal element to the extent of assassinating a sheikh. He knew this case would take six months, long exclusive months, before the ACC admitted defeat and took him off it—a sheer waste of time in an otherwise useful existence.

He unscrewed the cap from the Teacher's bottle. He turned to the photofit sergeant. "Get me a paper cup from the bogs, sergeant," he said. And he added, ". . . It'll be the only useful thing you've done this afternoon."

He changed brands. He'd started in Scotland Yard on Teacher's. Now it was Bell's. He lay on top of the bed in his Hammersmith flat, watching the telly, picture only, sound turned off, watching occasionally, too, the level in the glass of his third large Bell's. On the telly, Panorama, one of the endless breed of Dimbleby's, jawing dark political portents at the greatly tolerant English public.

Sound was unnecessary. Doom-laden expressions were enough, with occasional cuts to maps of Africa or the Middle East. He'd hardly mulled that one into existence when the Dimbleby did turn to a map of the Middle East. Regan's eyes focused in on the bottom right-hand corner of the telly screen—the Persian Gulf. He wondered where Haffasa had hung out. He wondered when the hell he was going to face the fact that he was on this case and there was no way out. He reached for the bottle of Bell's and topped his glass to the halfway mark.

He thought of Carter, Detective Sergeant Carter, his assistant. Carter had been in court all day giving evidence against a six-foot seven-inch West Indian pimp who couldn't keep his girls and had turned to ripping off customers, stealing wallets and belongings, in a couple of twenty-four-hour sauna shops he ran. Carter had other things to do after court and had said he'd check into the Yard after nine. Carter had not been assigned to the Haffasa case. Regan ran through the possiblities of some ways to involve Carter in the case. If he was going to be screwed himself for the next couple of months, he'd like a joker like Carter to share the shit. But Carter would be too smart for that, would see the danger and hightail it. He was on his own.

He thought of food, then he thought about the autopsy of Harvey Cantwell's girl, and his stomach turned over a quarter revolution. He'd been nearly seventeen years in the Met CID, and had probably attended in that time over two hundred post mortems, but this morning's had been the worst. Harvey Cantwell had a girlfriend called Gloria Milan. She was an ex-stripper, twenty-eight. She'd died on Saturday. She'd been drinking and she'd taken some sleeping pills, not enough, as the autopsy suggested, to have indicated suicidal intent. Somewhere during Saturday night after the booze and pills she had felt ill. Getting out of bed she'd collapsed and fallen on the electric fire, which she had left on. By the time she was discovered, seven Sunday morning, by neighbors attracted by the smell, the middle part of her body had been thoroughly burned. Gloria Milan had a criminal record office file, gained from years in prostitution—and a cross-reference on her file to the boyfriend, Cantwell. A coroner's office check with Cantwell's CRO produced a note to the effect that in his long career in crime he'd occasionally done a few favors, with information passing to the Yard and, notably, to DI Regan of the Flying Squad. Regan was requested to attend the autopsy.

It had taken place at 6:00 A.M. at Paddington General Hospital. The pathologist was a small man called Arps. Regan had witnessed his examinations before, but nothing quite like this morning's performance. The man had dug about in the corpse and come across the burned kidneys. He'd beamed a grin at his cold-faced assistant and at Regan. "Just how I like them, crisp on the outside, under-done in the middle." He'd finished the autopsy and given Regan his verdict: death by natural causes, aided by alcohol and pills. Then he'd asked Regan, "What are the funeral arrangements?"

Regan had glanced at the mortuary card. The hospital had already been in touch with Cantwell for his wishes. "She's to be cremated."

Arps surveyed the burnt corpse. "There's a good chap,

11

tip her relatives the wink. The job's half done. They should get a discount."

Regan had gone on from Paddington General to the Wellington Clinic. Thank God Haffasa's death MO was not in question—otherwise he might have to attend another of Arps's sessions. St. John's Wood, bordering the Paddington district, shared the services of the ghoulish little pathologist.

The phone by the bed rang. Regan debated whether to pick it up. It could only be more bad news. He picked it up. It was Carter with bad news.

"Evening, guv. I hear you topped some fucking Arab this morning. . . ."

Regan let the opening remark fall into a silent void of its own making. He was in no mood for chat. Then he said, "Not me, George. Some other buzz."

"Why kill him, guv?"

"Shut up. What d'you want?"

"I hear they've got you breaking stones. It's SB. Got to be. How come you got lumbered?"

"Farce. It's an outside contract. Everything arranged over a coffee table in Geneva or Abu Dubai."

"Sounds a turd."

"Right. What d'you want?"

"I want to know that I'm not in it, guv. I want to hear you say it. I want to inform you with precision that I don't want to go down with your millstones."

"Hold on." Regan dropped the phone on the bedside table to deliver an electric-powered clout to Carter's inner ear, and emptied some more Bell's into his whiskey glass. The gesture from the bottle to the glass rim was a little imprecise—some whiskey hit the carpet. Regan realized he was drunk. He took two gulps, disapproving of them and himself, and resumed the phone. "George, you were saying . . . ?"

"I don't like the idea that you're home in your flat, guv. You're saddled with a bastard and I reckon you're sitting there with a bottle of Bell's, working out all sorts of demoniacal bother involving me. I'm telling you, I don't want six months up a cul-de-sac. I wasn't at the Wellington Clinic. I don't want to be saddled. . . ."

"George, in future say fucking sir when you're talking to me. . . ." Regan dropped the phone back in its cradle and pushed the whole lot onto the floor. He lay back in his bed and studied the Bell's. There was exactly, he calculated, eleven-fifteenths of the bottle left. Was that enough to sustain his ruminations for another hour before he passed out, or should he get up and get another bottle from his local liquor store? No, he decided, the quantity would last one more hour while he worked out a few calculations. If the ACC had decided to fuck him up for months to come, then he could be bloody sure that he was going to pass some of the aggravation on down the line. He began to ponder a number of candidates who existed, almost by definition, to be screwed.

He emerged from the twelve-hour untypical morass of self-pity at nine the following morning. Yesterday the passive victim, today he would make action. He would make it hot for a selected few. He boiled himself three eggs, sat down behind them, and, instead of reading his morning *Daily Mail*, started drawing up mental shortlists.

He was stuck with the Haffasa assignment, so in the spirit of the late Bernard Law Montgomery, he'd turn historical defeat into victory. He knew he'd lost Carter. The commander of the Flying Squad would be annoyed enough about losing his top DI to a pointless murder hunt, without also throwing in a leading DS for good measure. Of course, he could summon assistance when required, but it would not be top caliber. Carter was the only DS of his acquaintance in the Yard that he could rely on a hundred percent.

Four things to be done. Revisit the scene of the crime and talk to the chief scene of crime officer. Check whether the special enquiry had turned up the cabby that had driven the killer away. Check Interpol for anything on Haffasa. Then to the Bahrain embassy—but he'd have to organize a telephone introduction from the corridors of power before checking in there. Meanwhile gather a list of every passenger leaving Heathrow Airport from noon yesterday. Haffasa was killed at 10:45. The killer who took the cab could have been on a plane out of London by midday. The passenger lists from midday to midnight might produce ten thousand names. The lists would be irrelevant at the moment, but later on he might have the clue of a name to check against them.

He got on the phone and called Airport CID at Heath

row. The Met had recently taken over the London air-port, but for some reason a gruff-sounding sergeant suggested that if he wanted information-gathering of traffic lists, then there were some lads in West Drayton who'd sort that out faster than Airport CID. Regan thanked him coldly for nothing, phoned West Drayton nick, and got one of the DC's there. He was promised passenger lists delivered to the Yard within three hours.

Regan checked with the Yard. DI Herrick, recently of Number Nine Regional Crime Squad, now with Special Branch, had apparently been hanging around the scene of the crime at the Wellington Clinic. He located Herrick in Special Branch section. Herrick said there were a couple of items on the SOC worth a chat, and Regan said he would be into the Yard after a short detour to the clinic.

He took the Westway route through the morning rain and traffic to St. John's Wood. It was the fourth consecutive day of rain in London, not fulsome showers but just depressing, persistent drizzle with windshield wipers in the traffic crawl along the Westway all turned to low speed. Behind the wiped commuter windshields the gray faces as depressing as the weather. Regan's face similar, but thoughtful as he queued his way onto the Marylebone Road and took a left up Lisson Grove for the woods of St. John.

It was as if he had absorbed all the facts and now, in the slow process of degustation, was finding something in the mix that upset his stomach. It may have been something to do with the speed with which the assistant commissioner of crime had assigned him to the murder—simply on the basis that he'd taken an elevator ride with the killer. This was a Special Branch case. The ACC had told him that Haffasa was a VIP oil sheikh and political figure visiting England. So if Haffasa was so important, why wasn't he under surveillance by the Special Branch yesterday morning? Or was he? Was Regan now to be a fall guy for SB ineptitude? Or had Special Branch surveillance turned a blind eye while a guest with an M-38 made a brief appearance? Or were there other ramifications, as yet unmentionable, whereby Regan, the wrong man by his own admission for the job, had been put on the job? Had he been given the Haffasa killing solely because he wouldn't be able to solve it? And next, what to do with all these propositions? Go into the Yard and talk to his boss, Chief Inspector Haskins, or Commander Maynon? Haskins was four years from his pension, Maynon two. Haskins's shifting eyes would say, "If the ACC's put you on this bash for no good reason except a number one blowout, then get on with it."

He drove off the main road and turned his Cortina into the front entrance of the Wellington Clinic. He looked at his watch. It had been almost twenty-four hours since he'd last been here to tell Harvey Cantwell about his girlfriend's post mortem. He climbed out of the car into the rain. He looked up at the building. He didn't expect to find much here. It was almost as if already he knew a part of the score. Intuitively he knew somewhere along the line someone was ahead of him loading the dice. First he must overtake that someone. He shrugged his raincoat collar up and buttoned it against the wet and headed across the tarmacadam into the clinic.

The nurse was attractive enough to be disturbing. In the intimacy of the empty elevator bound for the third floor Regan felt the almost overpowering need to reach out and grab her huge tits, or run his fingers through her magnificent auburn hair. "I'm getting old," he thought. "Fantasies are taking over. She's probably a black belt in judo." The elevator pulled in at the third floor, and the beautiful nurse stepped out and pendulumed her hips off down the corridor. Regan decided she was one of those rare birds who look as attractive from the back as from the front.

They reached Haffasa's suite. The nurse produced a key and unlocked the door. She turned and smiled at Regan. "Shall I give it to you?"

"Yes, I'd very much like you to give it to me." Regan's voice low and hot with double entendre.

Her face dropped. She pushed the key into his hand and walked off high-headed down the corridor.

"Thanks," Regan said sharply. She didn't look back.

He stepped into the room. The place had been cleaned up by a bunch of British constables—everything removed including the mattress. And yet the room was still somehow untidy. Regan guessed the line of fire was from the door. The suite had a bedroom and a sitting room adjoining it, but it was entered by the bedroom door. So it was different from Harvey Cantwell's suite at the bottom of the corridor. To get to Cantwell's bedroom you entered through the sitting room.

Regan marveled at the punch of the M-38. The wall behind the bare steel bed frame had five deep cavities in it. It would have taken an Irish navvy an entire day with a bottle of Powers Irish whiskey and a masonry drill. Presumably two of the excavations were made by bullets that had passed first through Haffasa, terminating his A+ consumer rating, before they hit the concrete. The bullet holes had been chalk-circled on the wall by Herrick or his men. What was left of the bullets would of course be in the Yard's forensic laboratories.

Regan really wasn't interested in that kind of line. He'd come to the Wellington Clinic for one reason: to see if Haffasa's suite was in any way overlooked. Could Haffasa have been under routine surveillance by the Special Branch?

He crossed to the windows and studied the wet playing fields of Lord's, his eyes finding the buildings beyond. The suite on the south side of the clinic was curiously isolated. There were possible sight lines to the third floor from, say, a bedroom in the new Westmoreland Hotel at the bottom of Wellington Road or the building next to it, Lord's Towers, apparently built for cricket freaks, overlooking the stadium. Either sight line didn't offer itself as an easy surveillance roost, but Regan knew that the Special Branch had recently, at some cost to the nation, picked up the latest 500mm SMC's for their Pentaxes— sharp close-ups on photographic surveillance over half a mile. The SB could have had the suite under photo surveillance from Lord's Tower or the Westmoreland. Regan studied the two buildings. He was wondering, although it was feasible, whether it was likely. He came to no conclusions.

For the next fifteen minutes he looked in the suite for

bugs, either listening devices in situ or visual evidence of the one-time presence of a bug or bugs. He found nothing. He went to the window once more, stood there looking out into the rain, eyes defocused, trying to work over combinations of ideas. Then he stopped for the moment, struck by how odd it was that what he was in fact doing was trying to calculate the degree to which his brother officers in Special Branch were lying through their teeth.

The United Kingdom has had a Special Branch, meaning secret police, for over a hundred years. Currently there were about two hundred officers in the branch. Their base, like most U.K. specialist units, was the Yard. They were just plain cops, and a half dozen of them were Regan's good friends. Their business was the business of any country's secret police: they arranged security for important politicos, they infiltrated subversive organizations after defining secretly and within their own infrastructure such words as *subversive*. Regan didn't mind the guys, thought on the whole they did a good job—with the occasional and memorable slip. Why was it, then, Regan asked the low cloud scud back of Lord's Pavillion, why was he thinking that they were at this moment screwing, or trying to screw, him? He couldn't put his finger exactly on it. There was the too-obvious fact—the shooting of Haffasa was a prima facie SB case and yet he was assigned to it. Why? Most professional cops would say that the fact that Regan had accompanied the killer down the elevator was neither here nor there. The killer had to be traced by painstaking investigation—then when he was near to being nabbed, Regan could be brought in for positive identification.

He left the suite, found the attractive nurse again, returned the keys to the room. She was still looking angry, but circumspectly—she had placed him in the number of crude men of her acquaintance and found he was not so wanting. He thought if he could hang some chat on her for ten minutes he'd probably make headway. But then he didn't feel in the mood. He stepped out into the rain again and got into the Cortina. He drove out of the hospital and south toward Westminster and New Scotland Yard. There was a time element involved. If he could get to grips with just the first round of general inquiries on this Haffasa case, then he reckoned he'd hit the snag that would either stop the case and get him off the hook, or tell him the answers to the key question—why had the ACC shoved him on this ride?

He checked into the squad office on the fourth floor of Scotland Yard, told the sergeant on the switchboard to get him DS Carter, to trace Herrick, and to shut his mouth to anyone else that he, Regan, was on the premises. The sergeant found DI Herrick in Number Nine Regional Crime Squad offices. Regan left Flying Squad office and went on one of the longest corridor walks in England, three hundred yards of corridor at the bottom of which the RCS offices were housed.

Herrick was a tall Scotsman who smiled at the end of his sentences. Someone must have told him it improved his hang-dog face. Regan didn't know Herrick well, the odd nod in the Tank (the pub club within the Scotland Yard building), but he knew his reputation. Herrick was a good detective, probably too good a detective, which begged the question. Regan asked him the question. "Why have you been hanging around the Wellington Clinic?"

"Just wiggling my thumbs, idle," Herrick said, and smiled. "Come to my office."

He had a small office with a desk piled high with the junk of a half dozen cases pending, buff files with their CRO numbers and contents spilled out. "Sit down," Herrick said. He offered Regan a full Embassy pack. "You smoke?"

"I drink. The Tank's just opened."

"I don't drink." Herrick grinned this time.

Regan shrugged. "You mentioned some joke items on the SOC."

"A couple." Herrick didn't sound too interested.

"What?"

"First the gun. The M-38. The lab believes it was brand new. They say two things. The bullet sides have burn traces of molybdenum packing grease. The Remington manufacturers have only been using moly greases to protect the metalwork on new guns for the last six months. Also on the bullets, microscopic traces of metal scarf, you know, tiny traces of metal dust that results from machining. These traces are usually shot out of the barrel within the first clip fired."

"Add it up for me." Regan didn't see any significance in what he had been told.

"The point is that the serial numbers on barrel and stock had been carefully removed."

"Where's the M-38?"

"On a plane back to Remington in the States. A long shot to see if they can see anything about it that could trace its recent purchaser."

"More like a waste of time than a long shot."

Herrick gave a large, open smile.

"How much of the clip did the assassin fire?"

"Half."

"Any markings on the clip?"

"Lab says nothing interesting. But phone them." Herrick reached for the phone.

"No, later," Regan said.

Herrick was already talking into the phone. "Sarge, tell Superintendent Maynon, squad office, that DI Regan is leaving me now and on the way to him. . . ." He replaced the phone.

Regan gave Herrick a long, poisoned look. "I didn't want to see Maynon."

"That's what the super told me."

"Thanks for fuck all," Regan said.

"Anytime," Herrick offered, and the hang-dog face split into a final seraphic smile as it witnessed Regan stamp out of the room and slam the door.

"Sit down, Jack."

Maynon was fifty-one. He had made it to the rank of superintendent, Flying Squad, at forty-three. That was young—and there was a reason. He was a very clever man. He had been a brilliant and active crimebuster for the first twenty years of his police life. Then he'd done what most intelligent cops do, mellowed into a thinker rather than a doer. There's every reason for crime, and a specific reason for each individual crime which can be mostly thought through. It *is* possible to sit in that consulting room in Baker Street and solve the bones of it with the odd excursion in a hansom cab into London fog. Over the last five years Maynon had reached that state. He would sit in his desk job in the Flying Squad office, inscrutable and few-worded, but mind working overtime. In the twenty-three years of his police history he had been associated with the detection of some of the most headline-catching crimes in the metropolitan district.

Regan sat.

Maynon took up his pipe from his empty "In" tray and lit it with a couple of Swan Vestas pressed together. He studied Regan through the smoke. "I've had some flak about you. . . ."

Regan gave a noncommittal shrug.

"The Haffasa case. Most folk round here when assigned a roving commission on a murder grab it. What's the headache?"

"You know," Regan said quietly.

"No I don't." Maynon's eyes narrowed, either the beginnings of anger or the intensifying of concentration.

"The assistant commissioner crime puts me on a Special Branch case. There has to be a reason. I don't mind politics. But I have to be told the score. So who's telling? I don't want to waste two, three, four months pissing against a solid brick wall for who knows whose amusement. . . ."

Maynon let a silence grow onto the tail of Regan's outburst. At first Regan thought he was just assimilating his words. Then he realized the man was angry. "What's the first job you ever did on the squad?" Maynon asked.

Regan hesitated, put off his stroke by such an odd question. "I think I busted a felon by the name of Parker."

"Why?"

He didn't know what answer Maynon was looking for.

Maynon wasn't looking for an answer. "You nicked a tea leaf because you were obeying orders. What in fuck's changed, Jack?"

Regan had an answer. "I have."

"You'd be surprised how little. The odd scar, a wound, a touch of the mental blocks. You're the same loud bugger we ever knew. You're at a dangerous age, Jack. You know, you're getting on for a squad cop, thirty-six and a DI still."

"With a difference. I'm the best DI in the squad. And the record to prove it . . ."

"Everyone knows you're a genius. I'm saying something else. You're getting on, you've seen it all, and you think you've put it all together. Well, I don't think you have. I don't think you've got all the subtle nuances together yet. Okay, the ACC has put you on a murder case that smells of the SB. I happen to know there are people in this building who think you shit gold bars. I think the ACC's put you on this case because, for reasons you'll have to right guess, he doesn't want the Special Branch dominating it." Maynon stopped there; his pipe had gone out. He pulled out two more matches and struck them. "When are you going to bloody wake up?"

Regan didn't have an answer. He wouldn't have given one anyway, because his mind was on the proposition, working it out. Of course Maynon was right. Haffasa, a VIP oil sheikh visiting London, would definitely be surveillanced by the Special Branch. So if they were watching him, how come he got topped?

"Were the SB watching Haffasa?"

Maynon shrugged through a cloud of pipe smoke.

Regan was quiet a moment. Then he said it. "Why would they lie, sir?"

Maynon was puffing in vain. The pipe went out again. He examined it—the tobacco had gotten too damp or too packed. He decided against the cleaning and refilling process and put it back in the "In" tray. "I think there are two sets of answers in this case. The given ones and the real. Start at the Bahrain embassy. Why did Haffasa come to this country? Who did he meet? Why did he go to the Wellington Clinic? Who did he see there? What are his politics, background? What part does he play in the international oil Mafia?—for instance, he's not a prominent name in OPEC. What's his private life about—did he live any of it in London . . . ?"

"I know the questions to ask, sir." Regan stood up. The interview was over.

But Maynon was doubtful. "Do you? On second thought I'm not sure I do. I don't like the idea that an Arab dies, and the SB is deathly silent, and the ACC is suddenly giving you orders. I think you got a big one on your hands, Jack."

Regan shrugged, turned, and walked to the door.

"Stay lucky," Maynon said gently.

Regan walked out.

He was followed. It didn't worry him. He was followed from the moment he left the Yard, walked to Victoria Street, and hailed a cab. It was 2:00 P.M. His lunch had been four scotches alone in the Tank waiting for a friendly face. There had been a lot of faces, none of them friendly.

Maynon was right. At thirty-six he was aging. A few years ago it would have worried him that he was being followed—now, nix to it. People who follow you are not usually a danger; they put that up front, like the don't-get-well greetings Haffasa received from the M-38. Besides which he was going nowhere private. The cab was heading for the Embassy of the State of Bahrain. The Bahrain lot, who with their other oil pals currently held Britain in hock, had not been able to offer an ambassador to lament with Regan the passing of the sheikh. They said they would provide a security vice-consul, whatever the hell that was, to answer or not answer the questions of the Scotland Yard detective.

The address of the Embassy of the State of Bahrain is Two Upper Brook Street, which is of course not an oil derrick's length from Claridge's Hotel. The embassy building is a restrained lump of Regency, and not too large inside. For coffee and games and general folderol the Araby sheikhs squat it out mostly down the road in Claridge's, almost as if they already owned the hotel.

The car that followed Regan was a Mercedes 280 SE

with two men in it. Regan took a couple of long looks at the car, through the smoked glass window of the cab, wrote down the license number, HJJ 51K, but couldn't see any details of the guy driving it and his squire. The Mercedes was sitting well back in the traffic.

As Regan stepped from the cab onto the pavement outside the embassy, the tail had tastefully disappeared. But Regan knew they would be back.

The embassy rooms were austere. The reception room looked like a busy Harley Street doctor's practice, with the same *Country Lifes* two years out of date. The room belonging to the security vice-consul was up-market from this, on the same floor. It was a cool green room, with a fine Bokhara carpet disappearing under some nice antique chairs and a Louis Quinze gilt ormolu desk.

The man behind the desk, the security vice-consul, when he rose to step forward and greet Regan, turned out to be a very large man indeed. The contrast was particularly marked because his Arab majordomo who took Regan from reception to the vice-consul's office would be about five feet three in shoes, which he didn't have on because he was wearing sandals. "Zehadim," the vice-consul said, extending a huge fist.

Regan extended his hand, expecting it to be crushed, but the man had a soft, brief handshake. He was quickly using the same hand to indicate for Regan to sit down.

Zehadim was six feet six, the type of bloke whose ancestors used to stand stripped to the waist, arms akimbo, at the door of the great man's harem, sword tucked inside support belt, with about a meter and a half of cutting edge honed to a turn. "Sit down, and would you like a cup of tea, Inspector?" Zehadim offered.

"Thank you, no," Regan declined.

"What can I do for you?"

"A little chat if you don't mind, about Sheikh Haffasa. I'm in charge of his case."

"I see," Zehadim said, with just an edge on the words.

"I'd like a curriculum vitae, dates, events of significance in his life. Names. I'd like a list of his friends, particularly in London, also in Bahrain."

"More appropriate, perhaps, would be a list of enemies."

"Of course. But it's from one's closest friends that you get a full list of the up-to-date enemies."

Zehadim smiled—a dark, brooding, mischievous smile. "A clever way of putting it. I'm not too sure I can help you there. You must understand Sheikh Haffasa was a bit of a recluse, a bit of a Howard Hughes. Though he was richer, of course. He was a private man. But there are some public things known about him."

"A question to you, sir. Have you any idea who might have killed him?"

"An unhappy, uncomplicated answer, Inspector Regan. No, I have no idea. No one here in the embassy has the slightest notion. We are all staggered by the news."

"You say he was immensely rich?" Regan asked.

"He was probably the richest man in our country."

Regan pondered the size of the huge man sitting behind the desk, the size of the fortune of Haffasa, and his own involvement. "How soon can you get me a list of his London-based friends?"

"My secretary will phone a couple of his best-known friends in London, and then hope that they can supply a list. Perhaps by the end of the day I'll be in a position to phone you at the Yard."

Regan stood. He didn't feel that this soft-spoken giant was going to be immediately forthcoming. He'd intended to keep the interview short. It was really just an introduction. Keep it short and he'd have an excuse to come again when he'd filled out more of the picture.

Zehadim didn't rise. From his position behind the desk he pushed his chair back. "One other thing, Inspector Regan."

Regan hadn't moved.

"Look. There are elements about Haffasa's death that you will be told about—but not by me. A plane comes into Heathrow 2200 hours tonight—a private job. On it will be one of our best detectives from Al-Manamah. His name, Europeanized, is Harry Hijaz. We will put him in contact with you. He will have ideas about why Haffasa was murdered. . . ."

"Does he think the murderer's in London?"

"Possibly," the man offered.

"May I meet his plane?"

"A Boeing 727. As I mentioned, Gate 18, Terminal One, ten o'clock."

Regan nodded.

"I don't promise that you will get anything out of Hijaz . . . he may not want to talk to you tonight. . . ."

"I see," Regan said. He was suddenly getting pissed off with the large man. He got up. "You'll be hearing from me." He moved to the door and turned. "This Harry Hijaz, does he have diplomatic status?"

Zehadim shrugged. "He's not a diplomat. The answer is no."

"Then if he lands on British soil with information, I assure you I'll get that information out of him. Good day," Regan said and walked out.

He went back to the squad office. The white Mercedes carefully trailed him to the junction of Dacre Street with Victoria Street, then disappeared. His speculation about the two men inside it didn't last long—he had plenty of other things to think about. But it did slightly worry him that he didn't care. He should have phoned the Yard from the embassy and informed a colleague about the white Mercedes and given its license number.

He walked through security and asked the two clerks on the hall desk if they'd seen Detective Carter. Yes, they said, he was in the building. Regan took the lift to the fourth floor and walked the squad corridor to the switchboard operator's cubbyhole at its end. "Harry," Regan addressed the man who was answering three calls simultaneously, "my DS is around. Find him for me."

Harry gave a vague look which sidled away. That signaled to Regan that he'd already been gotten at, that Carter had already visited and said something to Harry like, "Sport, my guv will be around soon. Make out you can't find me. There's a scotch in it . . ." The word would be all over Sweeney offices now that Regan had gotten lumbered with a dead-end case and would be looking for a mug to help share the load.

He went to his office, picked up the phone, and called Computer Bureau. A policewoman answered. "DI Regan, Flying Squad. Mercedes 280 SE, HJJ 51 K Kilo—can you run a check? Phone back any DS in the squad office with the brief to check full ownership. Yes, luv?"

"Yessir."

Regan replaced the phone. He didn't want to spend the time ferreting around investigating a car's ownership. He reckoned it would be a hired car. Let some DS find out who hired it, description of driver, check fingerprints on hiring receipts, documents, or car keys. That could be a whole day's work.

He sat down at his desk in his empty office and surveyed life on its last two days' rampage. Through the windows he saw the soaking vistas of polished slate roofs as the rain fell onto the great sponge of London. It had reached the point where it had started to depress him. A dark wet city and a lousy job. The Haffasa investigation was like the weather, poor visibility in every direction. But the story must have a profile and horizon. What had begun in the Wellington Clinic yesterday A.M. had not only a beginning, but a middle and an end. Next step, a Bahraini detective coming into Heathrow Airport on a private Boeing tonight.

Regan thought about Arabs—his attitude toward them.

He'd never really come up against them before, and now he knew he was going to be seeing a lot of them. It wasn't that he actively disliked them, but he housed some practical reservations about them. Two years ago, when his own world smelled of honeysuckle, he had sold his Ford Cortina and bought a Rover 3500. The Rover 3.5-liter engine did about eighteen miles to the gallon. Not too great, but just bearable on a DI's income. Then it seemed overnight the Arabs came along and doubled the price of petrol. Regan, who had conscientiously spent three years saving for his car, had to sell the bastard at the precise moment in history when all the other Rover 3.5-liter gas-guzzler owners were doing exactly the same thing. So he got FA for his example. Thus the Arab nations cost him actual bread, and pain, and puzzle. He couldn't understand it. Before Henry Ford invented the oil industry, these wogs had been experienced merchants selling their mothers, sisters, and other produce up and down the markets of Araby. How come the turbaned nits didn't realize their actions were going to threaten the currencies of all countries in the world, including their own? Or was it a conspiracy, had the Maoists infiltrated the harems, did they control those who were really running the shop?

And what did they want the money for, Regan had wondered in those days? There was a limit to Asprey's stock—you can only screw three or four high-class tarts at one time. So why wreck capitalism if the sole trick that interested those ex-tent dwellers and Elsan emptiers was the acquisition of material objects?

On the other hand, he had to admit, the Arabs made good waiters. Down the Mile End Road, there was a gyppo restaurant called Al Ahrain where three darkly good-looking brothers did a good hot dinner under £2.00, tax, VAT, and a large Bell's and a couple of lagers thrown in. So they weren't all bad—not every single one of the bastards.

He picked up the phone and dailed the squad switchboard. The operator answered.

"I told you, find Carter," Regan said heavily. "He is in the building, get him for me."

"Yes, guv," the ex-PC replied, and pulled the plug out on Regan before he could add anything more.

Regan took out his Benson & Hedges and lit one. He exhaled and studied the little patterns of smoke for a clue. So far there was just a shambles. Not a single thing that he could put his hands on.

The phone rang. It was the switchboard. "Guv, I've just heard Sergeant Carter has left the building."

"Thanks," Regan said bitterly, and threw the phone down.

It rang again. Regan picked it up and was about to shout into it. It was the Computer Bureau. "280 Mercedes HJJ 51K, Hertz—executive Rent-A-Car, St. James. Hired four days ago for a twenty-four-hour period. Hertz is anxious about the car."

Regan thanked the bureau, tapped the prongs, and asked the switchboard to find him a DS. The switchboard found him a DS Casson. Regan spoke to him. "Go to Hertz, St. James. Get the invoice on a Merc, HJJ 51K, place it in an envelope, bring it back to fingerprint. Get all other details of the hiring."

DS Casson said he would.

Regan replaced the phone. Nothing significant was going to happen until Hijaz checked in tonight, so why not see if he could make another contact with the white Mercedes that had been trailing him.

He checked his window again. Still persistent rain. He had a raincoat, but if he was going to walk, he'd need an umbrella. He contemplated from whom in the squad he would steal an umbrella. It was 4:30 now. The traffic would begin to thicken up soon, maybe not the best conditions for trying to corner the Mercedes. He hesitated a final time—the two men in the Mercedes were the only positive connection, however undefined, in this case. He should be making much more elaborate preparations for cornering the German car. If he fluffed a one-man operation, he might never see them again. He shrugged it off without resolving it. He walked down the corridor to DCS Hanley's room—Hanley was in charge of the property index at CRO, where all stolen goods are recorded. Regan stole his umbrella and headed for the bank of elevators to the street.

He walked down Dacre Street and turned right into Victoria Street. The wall of wet whistled and grabbed the umbrella almost out of his hands. These were no spring showers. On top of the soaking consistency of the weather it looked now as if the sinking British island was in for a cold snap—a nice place to visit but who would want to live there?

He studied the sour faces of the home-going, soaking the gale up through their spring dresses and lightweight suits—that would teach them. His eyes filtered through them, searching for threat. The men in the white Mer cedes could quite easily become two of these pedestrians by the simple *coup de théâtre* of parking their car. He walked mild-paced through the crowd, passed a Wimpy, and stopped to look in a Ryman window. He had gotten halfway down the street when he saw the Mercedes and the duo, tailing him through the traffic on the other side of the road. He had viewed them covertly and reckoned they wouldn't know he'd seen them. There were a number of options open to him. An instant's mental shuffle of the cards in the pack and he came up with the only one he wanted to play. He wasn't sure that he could single-handedly confront these guys, but he did want to know who they were, where they came from, and who had sent them. He needed a place with an entrance and at least two exits—plus a cab rank close by.

His pace quickened, but not too noticeably. He played the game casually, stopped for a second to buy an *Evening Standard* from a newsstand, and paused to read the headlines. He headed across the road, out in front of a darting Lotus and earned its horn, crossed Carlisle Place, and headed into the giant wind tunnel entrance of Victoria Station. He appeared to drop his paper, grabbed it, and took a look. The white Mercedes had braked on the corner of Vauxhall Bridge Road. The passenger in the car was out and sprinting toward him. Regan stepped out of the crush of people and into the first of the six entrance hallways to the main concourse. Then suddenly he was running. And everybody seemed to be getting in his way, and his elbows came out and he had to shove himself through English outrage.

The whole process of moving in the number one east

concourse door, hurtling through the protecting crowd, and out the furthest door three hundred yards away at the cab rank took less than forty seconds. Regan shoved his warrant card under the nose of a gray-haired businessman who was about to step into the first cab in the rank—behind the man, a long queue of commuters.

"Police," Regan shouted loud in his face. "I need this cab."

The startled man stepped back.

Regan jumped into the cab. "Police." He showed his warrant to the cabby. "Do as I tell you. Head down Buck Palace Road, left into Terminus Place, then up Wilton Road. . . ."

"Terminus Place is one-way, officer."

"Do it. . . ."

"What about insurance . . . ? What about an accident . . . ?"

"Do it."

Regan by now had dropped to the floor of the cab. He edged himself up to look over the door as the cabman reluctantly moved the cab forward. No sign of the man who had run from the Mercedes.

The progress from Buckingham Palace Road into the one-way Terminus Place was accompanied by a battery of motor horns and curses from his driver and from other road users hanging out of their cars, expressing how he was the wrong way up a one-way street. "Pull in here," Regan shouted through the noise.

The cabman gratefully pulled into the curb.

"Edge along to the corner."

The driver slowly trailed the cab along to the corner. Regan looked carefully through the window across the street to the top of Wilton Road. The Mercedes was still there, its driver at the wheel.

"See that white Merc across there?" Regan asked the cabby.

"Yes."

"It'll move off in a minute. You follow it."

"Could I hang the meter on, old man? Like I'm not a fucking charity," the cabman announced.

"Do that, son. You do that."

The cabman pressed the lever down and the meter started ticking.

"There you go," Regan said quietly. "When he gets in with the other one, get on after them."

The man who had followed Regan into the station was not sprinting now, though he was walking quickly across the stream of traffic to reach the parked Mercedes. The Mercedes's driver powered down his window. There followed a short chat with a lot of shrugging shoulders and waving hands, and then the guy climbed into the back seat, as if he was used to being chauffeur driven. Then the big car moved forward.

The cabman revved his diesel and headed out through a gap in the traffic to follow the Merc down Buckingham Palace Road.

"This is like bloody Kojak or somethin' . . ." he informed Regan.

"Fuck Kojak," Regan observed.

The Merc driver knew his London traffic and carved

his section of the road neatly from under the noses of the hundreds of other drivers heading north for the suburbs.

The Mercedes was not going far. Through Pimlico, up Sloane Street, through the park, and north for ten minutes.

Regan commanded the cabman to pull into the curb and halt. He paid him the fare, £1.05, and 10p tip, which was not overgenerous. And he didn't get out of the cab immediately. He was crouched down looking out into the rain, debating. The Merc had turned in and parked in front of the slope-sided building. The destination of the two men in the white car had been the Wellington Clinic.

Regan flipped through the possibilities. The cabman had turned and was looking at him coldly. "You staying here long, mate?"

Regan climbed out and slammed the door. He put the umbrella up. He started to walk the hundred yards to the clinic building. The cab took off, the cabman letting out some obscurantist obscenity drowned out by the vehicle's noise and muffled by rain.

Regan headed for the entrance of the clinic in Wellington Place. He started into the side street, was about to cross and pass between the stone gateposts and into the building, when suddenly the two guys from the Mercedes slipped out of the reception double doors and made for the white car. They either didn't see him or pretended not to—they appeared to be deep in a heated conversation. Regan quickly lowered the umbrella to obscure his face and changed direction down Wellington Place.

There were half a dozen people in the street, coming or

going from the clinic, but no cars. He heard the Mercedes start and rev thirty yards behind him as he headed down the pavement. He quickened his pace. The side street was less than a hundred yards long, was in fact L-shaped. He passed a parked maroon Jaguar. There was a chauffeur sitting in it, reading a morning paper through dark glasses. Regan reached the bottom of Wellington Place and turned right into Cavendish Avenue.

Cavendish Avenue, around from the Wellington Clinic, is a wide street containing some of the finest houses in London. One of these, halfway down, belongs to one of the Beatles. Their kind of bread put people in Cavendish Avenue, installed them in privilege and silence in a fine backwater, with well-swept roads planted in cherry blossoms now beginning to burst under the cold, spring rain. Regan walked over the first pink droppings, his pace quickening now. He wasn't quite sure of the geography of this immediate network of roads but felt his best move would be to circle the block and return to the entrance of the Wellington. By which time the Mercedes would probably be gone. He would have lost the Mercedes but he would be at least one move forward on the chessboard. Those guys must have gone back to the clinic for a reason.

He was about fifty yards down Cavendish Avenue when he heard the howl of engines followed by the high-pitched screams of tires. The two cars came lurching around the corner from Wellington Place. The Jaguar, which Regan had walked past and which had contained the chauffeur studying the morning paper, was in the lead. The white Mercedes was less than two yards behind. Both cars took the corner at over seventy and swerved on the loose-grit road, painting abstracts of black lines on it. Then they accelerated like the furies of hell were after them, and both bore down on Regan.

He ran. His feet pounding, fists bunched into his chest, squeezing out the energy, ran, hemmed in on one side of the pavement by the intransigent walls of the wealthy, built to keep intruders out, including those like Regan about to be swatted to death. This was exactly what was about to happen. That he was sure of. The Jaguar was coming for him. It had mounted the pavement a hundred yards away, torn a young, ten-foot cherry tree out by the roots, and now had a clear run in on its real target. Two and a half tons of Jaguar motor were screaming and sluing down the pavement to wipe him flat. What he couldn't be sure of as he tried to cover the last twenty yards to the garden door of the next house—which had a low wall that he might possibly be able to throw himself over—what he didn't know was the role of the white Mercedes. His lungs were tearing but he was not going to make it. He slowed almost as if he felt he should bunch his body for the impact. He heard the car behind him. He heard the crack of semiautomatic fire, followed by the scream of the tires of one of the cars suddenly altering course, then the Jaguar hit him, and he hit the wall, and he felt his hands, which were supposed to protect his face and head, scrape off most of their surface skin on the brick wall, then his head connected with the bricks, and he was down and only semiconscious.

He was kneeling, feeling the blood on his hands and his face—but it wasn't minutes after the impact, it was five seconds after the Jaguar had hit him, that he knelt there in Cavendish Avenue watching the two receding cars race away, unaccountably leaving him his life intact. He could see the gun in the hands of the passenger in the Mercedes. The guy was trying to fire into the Jaguar. The Jaguar was well and truly ahead now and disappearing around a left bend into Circus Road. The Mercedes hit a lamppost with a noise like an earthquake, sliced it off, and catapulted it in parts across the road. The Mercedes driver had tried to maneuver the car at an acute angle to the Jaguar so that the Mercedes passenger could get his rifle out of the window and pump shells into the maroon car. He'd partly succeeded. The Jaguar had dodged the fusillade of automatic shells, and in doing so had only clipped Regan instead of hitting him full on. But the Merc driver had partly failed. In making the maneuver the car had gone out of control, sliced across the surface of the macadam, and wrecked the lamppost before thundering off in further pursuit of the maroon Jaguar.

Regan knelt on the pavement and watched his two palms fill with blood. He knelt to get his wind back, to still the pacing madness of his heart, to close his eyes for one second and commit to memory the Jaguar driver's face, what he could visualize of it, and the license number of his car, which he had recorded in his mind—he would remember that. He knelt, holding his hands up, waiting for the shock aftermath to come and shake his body like a leaf. The pain in his hands came in pounding pulses. He held the palms of his wounded hands upward, like another crucified innocent. The rainwater pattered into his palms, diluting the blood into little streams that fell to the pavement.

The apartment had been professionally turned over. That is, real finesse had been shown in ripping the place apart; careful value judgments had been made of the same sort he would have made. The bastards who'd done it must have brought their own tools. They knew, like Regan knew, that it is not that easy to completely cut open two mattresses and unscrew the rear of the TV set. They must have brought a linoleum knife and a screwdriver, neither of which Regan had in his flat. They had also taken up the wall-to-wall carpet in his bedroom and gone through his one hundred paperbacks, throwing the lot all over the floor. They'd looked inside his electric kettle, percolator, toilet cistern. They had also kicked in about £40 worth of Japanese Imari pot which had served as an umbrella stand in the hall. Regan reckoned they did this because they didn't find what they were after. He was not disturbed by the loss of the Imari. He figured he might have ended up kicking it in from frustration, because there was absolutely no way he was going to work out what they wanted, and who the visitors were.

He put on the kettle for some tea, changed his mind, and painfully poured a scotch. He had come from the run-in with the Jag back to his flat in Hammersmith via St.

George's Hospital, Hyde Park Corner, where a nice Paki
M.D. did a fair job on his hand dressings and put some
awesome disinfectant on his head grazes.

He looked at the mess of the room, changed his mind
again and made the large scotch a larger scotch, then sat
down on the arm of a chair.

The flat had been left to him by his mother, who had
died three years back. It was not as if Regan had left it
exactly as it was out of blessed memory to her; he was just
not somebody who bothered about the material comforts
more than a roof over the pate, a gas ring for morning
coffee, and a comfortable bed for intercrural activities.
His mother had bequeathed a Spanish cleaner with the
flat, a lady of many talents, not including familiarity with
the English language, but she kept the place clean,
washed his shirts, always had a pint of fresh-ish milk in
the fridge, a bar of soap in the bath, paper in the bog, and
finally, blessings abounding, he never saw her. He left
her money out every Friday morning, and it was gone
when he got home. The last time he'd seen her was at his
mother's funeral at Hendon cemetery. Regan reckoned
that if he met her once she'd resign—otherwise she was
stuck with this bloody job because she couldn't tender her
resignation to someone who wasn't there. He wondered
what she'd think when she bowled in eleven ack emma
tomorrow and clocked this lot.

The scotch warmed him and found the little mental
mechanism which by now was probably holding a meeting of the nerve ends and saying they must all join
together in a protest and shake the bugger up for the near

miss one hour ago. Regan's body relaxed. His brain stayed fine-tuned.

If the firm that turned over this lot actually took paperback books off the shelf and went through them, ergo and etcetera, they were looking for something small enough, trim enough, to be hidden in the pages of a paperback. How about a piece of paper, or a letter?—he asked himself. The question was rhetorical—it had to be something like that.

He picked up the phone and dialed Scotland Yard. He asked for Special Branch and Herrick. The switchboard told him to wait. After thirty seconds, Herrick's voice purred into the phone. "Yes?"

"Regan. Listen." His voice was cold, sharp. "Somebody tried to kill me, near the Wellington Clinic. Maroon Jag MLN 405J. I won't bother you with a description of the driver. I've come back to my apartment in Hammersmith. It's been turned over. I've got a theory about it. I think you guys have set me up. I haven't had any contact at all with the opposition yet. You lot, I suspect, are in some way involved in this case, may well know the opposition. I think one of your pox-ridden colleagues has given out my address with some fucking outlandish fairy story attached to it. Now I don't mind that, if I know what the story is, but to set me up as target and not have the common courtesy to tell me from what direction the shots are coming, that's something else. . . ."

Herrick interrupted acidly. "All double Dutch to me, son. . . ."

"What's your problem? There's a joker in the pack. I'm

going to find him. I don't think it's you. You're not dumb enough to play this kind of hand. But somebody did, and I'm going to find him, and when I do I'm going to break his fucking neck. . . ."

Herrick may have had a reply, but Regan slammed down the phone before it got started. He didn't want a debate. He wasn't sure of his ground—not sure whether it was Special Branch. He was only sure of one thing, that he'd been set up for something right from the moment yesterday when the ACC had put him on this roving commission. But why set him up, and for whom? And what were the stakes if they were prepared, and they obviously were, to risk his life to get results?

It was 10:10, the night outside moonless and misty, and still the rain. Regan followed an airport security sergeant, who had a long stride, down the walkways in the basement of Number One Terminal in Heathrow Airport, through a couple of No Entry doors, heading for a ramp out onto an area of the runways. Regan had arrived at Heathrow at 10:00 exactly. He had been told on reporting to Airport CID that the Boeing had landed six minutes earlier. As far as they could discover, its single passenger hadn't left the plane.

There was a jumble of hardware on the square mile of cement apron, Boeings and Tri-Stars taxiing around in a howl of engines that made talking impossible. The sergeant stopped a couple of times to get his bearings.

Then he saw the plane and lengthened his stride again. By the time they had circumnavigated the terminal's out-buildings, dodged the ground traffic of petrol tankers and pickups, and reached the Boeing, Regan was out of breath. He had experienced this once before, that often, after shock, the heart is tired and it's no time to run the hundred yards in 9.57.

The Boeing 727 sat right on the edge of the parkway, navigation lights off, but the whole cabin blazing. The plane was painted yellow and black. There was no letter-ing down its sides, just the registration numbers on the tail plane.

The landing stairs were already in position. The sergeant mounted them, with Regan following. At the top, the door to the cabin was closed. For a moment the security man looked nonplussed. Do you knock on the door of an airplane? Or use the shortwave airport lapel radio/transceiver to call the captain that visitors are wait-ing on the landing stairs? The security man tapped on the door of the jet and looked even more put out when an Arab appeared at the window and waved him away. Regan tapped the security man on the shoulder; he knew the reason for the waving away gesture—the door would slide out a foot before hinging open. The Arab unlocked the mechanism and pushed the door open.

The security man turned to him. "I'll leave you, sir."

Regan nodded and stepped into the cabin.

There were three men in view. Two, including the guy who opened the door, were the stewards, their blue robes and red fezzes probably some kind of uniform. The third man, drink in hand, was standing by a leather couch across thirty feet of deep-pile white carpet. He nodded to Regan as he entered. Regan nodded back.

Regan started off across the carpet. He reckoned a very expensive interior decorator had been hired to produce a very simple effect. The regular inside of the plane, seats and overhead bag-and-coat closets, had been taken out, the shag carpet laid down, and the walls and roof lined with black leather. There were five couches, three of white leather, two of black. There was a long ebony unit running down one side of the plane. Some of its doors were open. It seemed to contain exclusively bottles of booze. There were cocktail tidbits in silver salvers on the top of the black unit. There was little else except a white TV set sitting on top of a custom-made unit incorporating a videotape machine.

The best item of decor was the man. He was beautifully made and perfectly clothed. Five feet ten, bronzed, good-featured face. The top of his head was quite bald, but this did not detract from the man's handsomeness. His athletic body was poured into the finest fit of £300 of Savile Row suiting; patent black shoes, subdued club tie, two plain rings on his fingers, and about £2000 of Piaget on his left wrist completed his wardrobe.

Regan gave a little bow, rather than offer his bandaged hands.

"Pleased to meet you, Inspector. My name is Hijaz," the man said, the voice soft, the English faultless. "May I offer you a drink?"

"Thank you. I'd like a scotch."

"There is a wide choice. A Highland malt, perhaps?"

"Laphroig?" Regan suggested.

Hijaz turned to flick his manicured fingers at the steward who had opened the door. "Laphroig whiskey. The bottle on a tray, ice and water." He turned back to Regan. "Please would you sit down."

Regan sank into the deep chrome leather. His host followed suit, took up a drink, sipped it, studied Regan—a decision for a moment of silence until Regan had a drink in his hand.

The bottle arrived on a salver, with a silver jug of water and a small ice bucket. Regan gestured to the steward that he wanted the scotch undiluted, without ice. The steward poured it. Regan raised the glass to his mouth and sipped. Laphroig was a woody malt. A rare drink for him, but sitting in this flying gin palace seemed to be a possible occasion.

"I heard of an attempt to kill you with a car. Are these bandages the result?"

"How d'you know that I was involved in an incident with a car this afternoon?"

"The airplane has radio communication. Obviously I have talked to your associates at Scotland Yard before arrival."

"What associates?" Regan tried to keep the edge out of his question.

"Come, Inspector, there's more important information for you to acquire."

"Explain yourself, Mr. Hijaz."

"I will. I will do it slowly, carefully. The story itself is simple, the additions and errata very confusing."

"Go on."

Hijaz sipped the drink and then looked into it, as if by studying the liquid he would focus his concentration. "Twelve months ago King Faisal of Saudi Arabia was murdered. You remember that?"

"Yes, by his nephew."

"The world was told he was murdered by his nephew— but that was because the Saudis did not want the truth out. Besides, they wanted to get rid of the nephew, a dangerous lunatic."

"Who murdered him?"

"The man who murdered Mr. Haffasa yesterday."

"What man?" Regan asked.

"A greedy man. He wants a lot of money."

Regan sighed. He knew Hijaz was going to turn out to be the kind of informant from whom every word would have to be dragged. "Could you explain that?"

"We have a parallel society in the Middle East. Kings speak to each other, sheikhs speak to each other across national boundaries." Hijaz shrugged. "Okay. This is what happened. In 1974 an unidentified man got into Faisal's palace in Riyadh, probably the most heavily secured building in the world, and not only took a potshot at him with a .38 revolver, but escaped, leaving no clues. Faisal and his entourage hushed the thing up."

Regan nodded. "Go on."

"A week afterward Faisal received a letter containing a bullet, identical ballistics, demanding a ransom of fifty million dollars approximately. Faisal's advisers told him to ignore the threat, tightened security, and nothing happened. At least, nothing happened for a year, then in

49

March 1975, Faisal was shot dead at a family meeting by someone who was seen for a second time and disappeared. The bullet that killed him had the identical ballistics of the original potshot. So far you are following?"

Regan nodded.

"A month after Faisal's death an intruder got through the inner ring of security at the Shah of Iran's palace at Tehran and took a shot at the shah, wounding him in the leg—a fact made public a few days later in Switzerland in the guise of a skiing accident. The assailant got clear of the palace. One week later a letter arrived from the assailant, enclosing a bullet of identical ballistics to the one pried from the shah's foot. The letter demanded a hundred million dollars for the shah's continued good health, and noted the foolishness of the late King Faisal for not taking such demands seriously." Here Hijaz broke off. He looked over Regan with a slight smile. "We all know the shah is not a very bright chappie. He pays a lot of money to his police operation. When they came back a few weeks later and told him they had collared the assailant, he believed them. A mistake. Now this guy plays a waiting game—he waited a year to kill Faisal. Meanwhile we know that he sent demand notes to two other rich persons."

"Haffasa?"

"Yes, I'm afraid. Sheikh Haffasa received a threat in Bahrain a month ago. He was due to go to England on a medical matter. He thought he would be safe in England and deal with the situation on his return. The assailant decided to move fast this time. Haffasa died. Maybe that was intended to be a lesson of *encourager les autres.*"

"Two notes?" Regan queried.

"He sent out two demand notes. The second arrived a week ago."

"Who?"

"The richest man in our country. Sheikh Mahomet al-Almadi. Head of an important oil family. On top of that he has a finger in every industrial and commercial pie. The assassin's note demands fifty million dollars. Almadi wants to pay."

"I see," Regan said.

"The demand note tells him to go to a hotel in the south of France . . . Antibes . . . and wait there for instructions."

Regan was nodding slowly.

"It's possible you've seen this man, in the elevator at the Wellington Clinic."

"I saw a killer. Does he write the demand notes or is he an agent for the man or organization which writes them? I wouldn't know. What are your ideas?"

"To invite you to holiday in the south of France. I have already gained permission from your superiors. We hope that you will recognize the face in a crowd when a man comes to collect a lot of money from Almadi."

Regan shrugged, reached forward, took the bottle of Laphroig, and replenished his glass. Then he studied Hijaz for a moment in silence. "Eats on this plane?"

"We have a kitchen. Anything you want."

"A little food. Enough to sustain us for two or three hours. That's how long it may take for you to sell me the bill of goods. You see, from my understanding of this case, I don't see any reason to believe anything you've said."

Hijaz said nothing, then started to nod, like he had decided Regan's statement was very wise indeed. "All right, where do we start?"

Regan had an answer. "Let's start right here. Something I expect to get a straight answer about. Who are you? Just who the hell are you, Mr. Hijaz?"

He said his family came originally from Lebanon. He had five years' schooling in the American School in Beirut. His father was an Iranian, his mother half French. His father had started as a carpet salesman and ended up an oil engineer. He was shot dead in a barroom fight in Basra. His mother had taken him into the household of a wealthy man in Bahrain. He had failed every school examination he'd ever sat. Therefore it occurred to him, he said with a slight smile, to become a policeman. Strings were pulled, and he entered the State of Bahrain CID. He quickly gained promotion to captain. However, he soon lost interest in family feuds and camel rustling—five years ago he had moved into the semi-state, semiprivate employment of arranging security for the top twenty men in the country—the group known as Al-Manamah. Regan had asked him to explain that. Hijaz said the state gave him a policeman's salary and status. The twenty men added the gratuities that made life bearable. He said that it was a full-time job keeping those twenty alive.

"Where do you think the country of origin of the contract artist might be, the man who actually killed Haffasa?"

"You saw the man. What was his skin color like? His complexion? His hair?"

Regan hesitated. "The man who went down in the elevator with me could have been a European."

Hijaz nodded. "Yes, we think he could have been European. More than that, and the reason why I'm here . . . I happen to believe that the whole blackmail-threatening operation is staffed and run from London."

They were in a Rolls-Royce Phantom V heading into the after-pub race of traffic around Hyde Park Corner. It was an official Bahrain embassy car, chauffeur driven by a fifty-year-old Egyptian. This man had gotten Hijaz through Customs at Heathrow with a couple of smiles and a few words, even though the Bahraini policeman was not traveling with diplomatic status. Regan wondered how.

Their destination, Hijaz had told him, was the Hilton. "I love the London Hilton because all my friends detest it. I can sit there in peace. You will come to my suite. We will talk about this case. We are in a similar position, Mr. Regan. For the moment my focus is London. I am unfamiliar with the workings of the city. You are unfamiliar with motives for Haffasa's end. . . ."

"You say he died because he didn't pay protection. . . ."

But Hijaz now shrugged. "I like everything in black and white. But let us not run out of gray. I have been a policeman too long to rule out the gray areas in everything."

Regan didn't realize the floors contained that number

of rooms, didn't know that a suite could go around three sides of the hotel. To get to the dining room, he had to follow Hijaz, the chauffeur and butler and maid through rooms and corridors that were all part of a single suite.

A quarter of an hour later they were seated in the private dining room, starting on the meal which had already been in preparation as they headed into London. As Regan and Hijaz had just eaten some salmon and beef sandwiches on the plane, they modestly ordered a couple of plain omelettes.

"When do you retire each day?" Hijaz asked him.

"When do I go to sleep? Around two A.M."

"Fine," said Hijaz. "D'you like girls?"

"I like girls."

"Good," Hajaz decided. "We will telephone some girls. I know charming English roses. But tomorrow we must be up early."

"What line d'you want to pursue tomorrow?"

"The two gentlemen in the white Mercedes. Who are they? When you followed them they went back to this Wellington Clinic—why? That's where to start. If we identify them, we identify another target, the man in the Jaguar who took exception to you. . . ."

"Captain Hijaz, do you know if your embassy called in the English Special Branch for Haffasa's visit to London?"

"I understand our ambassador has said no—he didn't call in the SB to protect Haffasa. But in view of what happened I think he may just be giving a diplomatic answer."

"I'll start with the Wellington Clinic. I want you to try

and find out about the Special Branch. You see, in normal circumstances, whether they were called in or not, the SB would have checked on Haffasa's security. So if the guy dies, there's something wrong there—d'you understand what I'm saying, Captain Hijaz?"

Hijaz nodded, took his time, and swallowed some food. "I am following exactly what you say, Inspector Regan. And I find that idea particularly interesting."

He remembered some beautiful girls, four, or maybe five. He remembered he and Hijaz had gone to the Playboy Club and queued up with all the other sheikhs to piss good money away and that he, Regan, watching the horrors of capitalism gone mad around him, for repressed left-wing political reasons only, drank himself into a stupor and incredibly made good progress with the best-looking bunny in the bar. But the four or five girls didn't come from the Playboy, or the Saddle Room, but somewhere else—a Frith Street club, which had cost the Duke of Edinburgh's wages to get into, and was called Privé Numero Un, and was furnished by soft lights and terrific broads. They all appeared to be debutantes. Regan in his cups found the fair logic to that. Debutantes were really whores—squired by rich daddies and richer mummies through the salons of dying Belgravia, paraded like cattle, screwed, approved, and married to the impecunious with the decent names. Or the exact opposite, the debutante daughters of impoverished aristocrats were offered around Belgravia to make a match with a millionaire scrap merchant in order to improve his family's "breeding." How natural it appeared to Regan's besottedness that these long-legged, hoarse-voiced lassies, raised on silver spoons of Meusli at Roedean girls' school were now balling their way to the top on, or under, sheikhs, freaks, and the businessmen in Frith Street. Hijaz was well known at Privé Numero Un. He told Regan he hadn't been to this bluestocking bordello for over a year. He was known, all right. He paid for everything immediately from a six-pack roll of brand-new bank notes. He was known and loved. He danced on the newspaper-sized dance floor with three of the loveliest hanging on to him.

Regan enjoyed every second of it. It was true the point of no return had passed by 2:00 A.M., and now the brain fluids were so diluted by alcohol that all great thoughts and resolutions had been thinned out. He was floating, but it was a happy, heightened sensation, time had lapsed, he was anesthetized. The music was fast and fresh, the girls so desirable, wanting to be loved, but it was all down to the art of the possible, and he felt it was not anymore. He could hardly stand. He knew there was fresh air out there in Frith Street, and when he hit it, the dreaded Father Mathew, scourge of alcoholics, founder of the Anti-Alcohol Pioneer Movement, would crap down on him from the great height of a Heavenly Throne. His eyes started to see double around 3:00 A.M., but he did make it to the street, to the Rolls-Royce Phantom V, to the door of his apartment in Hammersmith, and he kissed many girls on his way and felt parts of them, and was happy. And Hijaz promised him there would be a replay.

Hijaz got that wrong. The following morning Regan's phone blew out both his eardrums at nine. He was in the bedroom of the Hammersmith flat, on the bed, not sleeping, still comatose. He picked it up very slowly. "Yes?"

"Good morning. Harry Hijaz."

Regan vaguely remembered last night and meeting this man, all his memories fighting for recognition above the pounding pain of his hangover.

"I will come to your apartment in half an hour. Please be packed—we go to the south of France. . . ."

Regan let the news percolate and bubble around his hangover brain. "I thought you said the south of France in a few days from now. . . ."

"Almadi is arriving in Antibes a few days ahead of schedule."

"We have investigations to do here. Essential groundwork. The Wellington Clinic, the SB angle."

"The sheikh is arriving in Antibes. The living come before the dead. You are the only man who can positively identify the killer."

"What is your sheikh doing, coming earlier to Antibes?"

"He has a meeting to attend."

"Get him to cancel the meeting."

"It's an important meeting. With the French foreign minister."

Regan caught sight of his booze-battered face in the mirror. "It'll take me longer to get organized. Maybe a couple of hours. I have to ring F3, get tickets and expenses. And call the central office and get them to warn Interpol I'm coming."

"That's all been done, old man," Hijaz said cheerfully. He had drunk only two whiskeys the whole of the night. "Say forty minutes." He didn't wait to hear Regan's response. He replaced the phone.

Regan got out of the car and stood still, surprised at the heat of this sun on a March day. The sky, facing out to sea, clear. The sun stripped of haze, hanging like a medallion awarded to the Mediterranean by the French Tourist Board. Behind Antibes the inshore breeze touched the mountains with wisps of cotton and hard shadows. The visibility was at least thirty miles.

He remained by the car, reluctant to move. He wanted to feel the warmth for a moment, its benediction on his arrival. He wanted to soak in the silence of the vast gardens—a silence as tangible as its surroundings—the wide plateau of lawn, the thousand trees, and the sea edging the peninusla, protecting stillness like a wall.

Hijaz and the chauffeur had gotten out of the car. They exchanged quiet monosyllables as if they had no wish to bother him.

Regan looked out to sea. A mile out, a small boat white-knifed the water. Then he turned and looked back to the fastness of the hotel, green shutters framing a hundred blank windows. His glance went over the other cars around him. One Maser, two Ferraris, and a half dozen Mercs. Hôtel du Cap, Eden Roc, this place was called. Hijaz said this hotel on its own hundred acres of private promontory, with the famous Eden Roc Club, was expensive. Regan was prepared to believe that, as distinct from everything else these lunatic Arabs had so far told him.

He turned and followed the chauffeur and the Bahraini across the fresh grit tarmacadam and up the steps, through the doors, and into the wall of cold air guarding the hotel lobby.

Reception appeared poised, waiting for them as if they had been expected all morning. In the next few minutes they made their processing under the roof somehow an event of significance, but also discreet. The Hertz chauffeur who had driven them in from Nice Airport spoke little English. Hijaz, it turned out, spoke French like a native. There was some formal talk in both English and French about the impending arrival of Sheikh Almadi. What time would the sheikh be arriving? Should they send a car for him? No, Hijaz said, there would be several cars prearranged at the airport—he was arriving between five and six.

"If you would require anything, you must not hesitate to ask. . . ." the senior clerk addressed Regan. But Hijaz nodded to him, well acquainted with the formalities, as if he'd spent his life booking into hotels. He turned to Regan.

"Would you mind to go ahead to the suite? I do have details to discuss with these gentlemen."

Regan nodded and followed a bellhop up the white stairs.

The bellhop bowed him into the suite. There were

signs and smells of the place just having been cleaned—lavender polish and bath scour. He went to the French windows, two sets with two balconies, and opened them wide.

Silence trapped in the still air, no movement on the lawn spreading out to fringe the cobalt water. The colors of the garden were slightly shrill to his eyes.

He was aware of someone behind him and turned. There was a frizzy-haired man, middle-aged, with a tray of scotch, demi-bottle of Evian, and ice in a second glass. Presumably a present from Hijaz. He gestured to the man to put the tray down on a massive escritoire. The waiter went out silently.

He turned to his scotch on the tray. He put one ball of ice into the glass, then topped up with a lot of Evian. He sipped, and felt the fatigue soak into him as his body relaxed. He stared out of the window to the view of the sea again. "What the fuck am I doing here?" he asked himself, half aloud, and he suddenly realized it was a real question and not rhetorical.

He heard the door close and Hijaz was standing there. "You like it? Nice hotel, eh? Classy views." Hijaz moved over and took up a stance at one of the open French windows. "Place looks good." His eyes on the gardens, clipped lawns, and high trees, the look of a businessman who has just bought the hotel. "When was the last time I was here? Two years. It never runs down, this hotel. The buildings, the grounds, like they have just been freshly laundered. Charming."

Regan pondered. "I'm studying the layout from the point of view of an assassin's bullet."

"Relax. We don't have to worry for a few hours until Almadi comes."

Two porters entered with the suitcases, eight of them. Seven belonged to Hijaz, one was Regan's. Hijaz directed the porters to take his luggage up to the Almadi suite. The phone rang. Hijaz went over and picked it up. He said one oui into it and put it down. He turned to Regan. "Rejoice," he said, "the crumpet has arrived. . . ."

Sheikh Almadi had sent his girls on in advance—six of them. The stay in Hôtel du Cap was not scheduled to last more than a week. It didn't have the formality of an official visit, so he didn't bring his wives. The girls were all European, three French, two German, and an English girl named Jo. Regan had met her at the nightclub in Frith Street. He had forgotten her. She had remembered him.

They arrived in three cars. They all knew each other from Almadi's regular sorties in Europe. Regan had a problem believing his eyes. They were all extremely beautiful. It was like a fantasy from a tit mag. The sheikh and the retinue of pretty girls. And then the extension of that. These girls were not here to decorate the foyer of Hôtel du Cap—these were working girls. They all knew each other. So what was the work?

They arrived in the hotel between 2:00 and 3:00 P.M. Hijaz met them, embraced them, was not too sure about each of their names, but introduced them and laughed when they corrected his pronunciation. Regan was introduced as "a very important policeman from London."

"You on duty?" Jo asked.

"No," Regan said. "You come here often?"

"We met in London," she said. "Privé Numero Un. You don't remember?"

He shook his head. Alcohol had stepped between the projector and the brain screen that night.

"You raped me in a Rolls-Royce with six other people in it."

"Is that possible?"

"Not sure, but you certainly tried. I remember we dropped you off at an engine shed in Hammersmith where you said you lived."

"I don't remember."

"I remember you were funny."

Regan said nothing, gave a smile. She was lovely. The mistake would be to rush fences. He had to find out what the hell was going on—six girls and a sheikh. He caught himself shaking his head in a mimic of mild Victorian disapproval as the lovely girls spilled in and out of reception, sorting out their room numbers within the Almadi suite, arranging for baggage to be brought in from cars, all this under the quiet no-questions stares of the hotel staff. Then he caught himself further along the extension of his thoughts. There was no doubt who was the prettiest of the six—Jo. Twenty-two to twenty-four, tall, straw-colored blonde, fine silk hair. She was not at all the shape that Regan's dad would have gone for—no tits or arse, built to an age of compromise and sexual ambivalence. Regan's dad would have said her legs were too long. Regan's eyes followed the length of them tight in Newman jeans, and his mind speculated on long nights and the spaces between. A face like an adolescent boy, but a young girl's full lips. Blue, mildly worried eyes, even when she laughed—a girl who had probably run a gamut of problems and worked them out enough to remain reasonably intact. Her voice, just like the other girls of Privé Numero Un, Buckinghamshire County Council, Cordon Bleu cookery classes, nil academic attainments, but despite that, bright. She laughed a nice clear laugh, had a sense of humor about this situation. Here she was in a bunch of international call girls, all here to wriggle their fannies at some old fart.

Hijaz had said Almadi was sixty years old. Was he also a perfectionist, in which case he must give the major part of his attention to the English Jo, or was he decrepit, short-sighted, gone blind with too much of it, in which case Jo might have spare time? The half dozen sentences she had said to Regan implied that she might be interested in him, given a little encouragement.

The girls took twenty minutes to settle everything, dispatch their luggage to the suite, and redo their makeup. Then they all decided they were hungry. They strolled down toward Eden Roc. The desk clerk had told them the restaurant would stay open for an extra half hour. It was 3:10. The gardens were empty apart from the sound of the girls and their laughter, and the plopping of some tennis balls hit by unseen players behind screens of herbage.

They went into the Pavillon Eden Roc.

There were six late lunchers still eating. And too many

waiters talking in low voices to each other as they busied themselves doing nothing in a series of fast, ferrying trips around the sea of empty tables.

Hijaz ordered the table for eight, then stood about like a mother hen telling the girls where they should sit. Regan ignored him, and when Jo sat, he sat down next to her.

Regan looked at his menu. It all looked exotic. All he wanted was something light, grilled, plain. He had to work this afternoon. He turned to Jo. "Tell me, what do you and your pals do for this old sheikh?"

"We mind our own business." She said it like she meant it, her eyes not leaving the menu. Then she relaxed and looked up. "I'll have some lamb navarin." Then she said, "Almadi's nice. He likes us to run around without any clothes on. He's pretty uncomplicated. He has simple tastes. He likes a bit of a cuddle and a feel. Seldom more. Got it?"

Regan nodded without committing himself to approval or disapproval. "How much d'you get paid for this . . . ?"

Her laugh was open and ironic. "You expect an answer?" Then she shrugged it off. "The answer is he's very generous. I turned down four days modeling on a big new Chrysler model launch to be here." She smiled again. "What does he pay you . . . ?"

"I'm on Met CID overseas per diem. Eight pounds fifty a day plus reasonable traveling allowances."

"What are you doing here?"

"Acting as a security adviser for Almadi."

"He's as secure as the Bank of England. What's your Christian name?"

"Jack."

"It is beautiful weather, Jack. I think you and I are going to have a nice time."

At the end of lunch they all trailed back to the hotel. Jo found the gravel hot to touch. She had taken her shoes off, tied the laces together, and slung them over her shoulder. "Let's go for a drive."

Everyone agreed. It was still several hours before Almadi arrived. They would go up for the best view of the coastline. Hijaz chose three of the girls and led the way in a Mercedes. Jo announced she would take the other two. Regan did not get a specific invitation to join them in the little Hertz Simca. But he went over and sat in the front seat next to her.

They headed off, the Simca trailing the Merc, up the coast road to Nice, through the vacant preseason city and around the back onto the Moyenne Corniche. It took half an hour to navigate up onto the Grande Corniche and up again to the crystal air of Eze—then in five minutes down from Eze to Les Hauts for the Hollywood view of the Côte d'Azur. Two miles below the white piano keys of the new tower blocks of Monaco mixed in with the minarets of original baroque, and thirty miles visibility of the coast and the resorts stretched in each direction.

The girls spilled out of the cars and moved through the tall grass. One of them had a Frisbee, and it passed around spinning high and awkward from the gusts of wind below. One of the French girls had lived in Menton some years back. She said she knew some beautiful and attainable men there, and after Almadi had returned to Bahrain she would go to Menton and not sleep for a week. There were catcalls, and Hijaz threw the Frisbee to bump her on the head. Regan wandered through the rocks and rye grass down to the edge of the cliffs. The drop was spectacular—the first drop an almost perpendicular fall of fifteen hundred feet. He heard footfalls in the rocks and turned. Jo was coming through some gullies to join him.

"Beautiful," she said of the view.

"Right."

"What a day."

"It's cold."

"It's sunny, after the filth of England these last few weeks."

He kept looking at her. "Why are we talking about the weather?"

"What else shall we talk about?"

He shrugged.

She laughed, a feminine laugh, no nervousness or fake pretension. "You name it."

"Okay, when do we get together and fuck?"

She made a little biting gesture of her lips, working it out. "I've never met a detective before."

"Is that good?"

"I don't know." She looked out across the fall of land to the blue water, and farther to the soft blue horizon. "What are you doing with Hijaz and this Almadi group?"

"There have been some attempts against certain people's lives. Almadi is known to be a target."

"Seriously?"

"Yes."

"How interesting." She sounded like she meant it.

"I was working on a case in London. They've shipped me down here."

"Probably not tonight, maybe tomorrow."

"What's that?"

"The answer to your question."

He took her hand, studied it, and was silent for a moment. Then they turned and walked up the pathway through another group of rocks and around and back to the cars.

On their return to the hotel the group split up to prepare for Almadi's arrival. Regan went to his room and put in a call to Scotland Yard. He asked for Chief Superintendent Maynon. Maynon's voice came on the line. He sounded tired. "Yes, Jack. Anything to report?"

"Good food, digs, nice gardens, girls, not necessarily in that order."

"Almadi?"

"Not arrived yet. But the pillow talk's organized. I'm not invited. I can't understand how people who lay on orgies always get prudish at the idea of an extra guest. . . ."

"Have you anything to report, Regan?" Maynon's voice irritated.

"Yes. There is a point to this call. Just to remind you, and the ACC, and the Special Branch, and any others involved, that I still reserve my position. If I find out that I'm being led up the garden path by Special Branch, you, or anyone else for whatever reason, then I'll be giving you a lot of problems. . . ."

"Goodbye, Jack," Maynon said, and put down the phone.

Hijaz knocked on Regan's door at six o'clock. Regan opened the door. The Bahraini stepped in and crossed to the window and looked out as if he expected to see something or someone below. "What do you want to do tonight?" he asked.

"I'd like to talk to you and Almadi about security. I'd like to check the hotel by night. . . ."

"Check it, how?"

"From the point of view of someone walking in with a gun."

"What sort of discussion do you want with Almadi?"

"I want to know his movements for the next two days. I'd also want to describe to him the killer I saw in the Wellington. I'd like to see if I can get him thinking about anywhere in his life he might have met the guy. Questioning people is the Pandora's box—sometimes they turn up answers they didn't even know they had. . . ."

"Jack, don't press to meet Sheikh Almadi tonight. He has many matters to attend to. Tomorrow morning would be a good time."

Regan wondered about that and decided he didn't really care. If Almadi wanted to give himself a coronary with one or all six of the girls and save the assassin a bullet, then that was his own business. Although he would shortly make sure that the sheikh's suite was as secure at night as by day. At the same time Regan felt it was a pity that his own attitudes were so unsympathetic to these people. He couldn't really get worked up about the idea of someone potshotting at sheikhs. Did it matter—was it relevant to him, his life, his career in London as a Flying

68

Squad detective? "Wish him joy on the many matters he has to attend to. The morning will do to meet him."

"Ten A.M. For one hour. The French foreign minister is to see him at eleven."

"Fine."

"Will you have dinner with me later tonight?" Hijaz asked.

"Certainly."

"Say eight-thirty?"

"Fine."

The broad-built Bahraini started moving to the door. Regan stopped him. "Hijaz."

"Yes?"

"I like the girl Jo. Would she get into trouble with her employer if she spent a few hours with me?"

"I'm glad you raised the point," Hijaz said coldly. "When Almadi pays a great deal of money for his women, he doesn't like being taken for a ride. Jo is his favorite."

"So bugger him," Regan said quietly.

Hijaz shrugged and walked out of the room.

They made love. The bed was by the window, and the stars looked down. She had a great physical passion but she used it subtly so that Regan felt he was offering as much to her as she to him. He paced her needs, learning that she found love a violent thing and that she could take more than the deepest thrusts, and then more. She stopped him once, not just for simple want but real need that it last longer. And in the end she was crying, but not from pain or failure, but because she was happy and holding him hard into her beautiful body because she could not let him go.

It was midnight; somewhere a clock in the hotel made truncated chimes, not a dozen of them. Regan counted six as he held her and studied the stars. Out there the moon retreated and the blanket of the night covered over the aftermath of sweet mysteries. Regan alarmed to find such a girl, worried at the exotic circumstances in which he'd found her, because he now saw it as unlikely that this sudden love could transfer back to London. And he wanted that, as he wanted her. And he scanned his memory over the dozen beds and couplings of these last years since his divorce, and he could not remember any woman who had loved and remade him like this girl Jo had done tonight.

She asked for a cigarette. He climbed from the bed and found her bag and opened it. He took out the Benson & Hedges and lit two. He took them back to the bed and climbed in. Her left hand moved and found a resting place between his thighs.

She had come to him. He'd had dinner with Hijaz after a thorough search and check of all entrances and exits, and locks and bolts and burglar alarms in or around the huge third-floor Almadi suite. Regan had concluded that the Wellington Clinic killer was not going to get at Almadi that night by any means, from highly subtle burglary to just walking in. Hijaz had suggested they eat in the hotel dining room. Regan had agreed. It had turned out an excellent meal and had ended at 11:00 P.M. with Regan

70

pleased and pissed. At eleven-thirty he was collapsed on his bed in his suite reading yesterday's copy of the *Times* nicked from the unattended kiosk below, when the knock came on his door. He'd opened it. She'd said, "The old man fell asleep. I got away." She'd said nothing else, from taking off her clothes to getting into bed and making love to him.

Some light filtered in under the door from the hallway. Regan watched her face on his pillow. She smoked a cigarette like a cigar—the occasional puff, not inhaling much. She seemed content, other-worldly after the intense energy of her lovemaking. There was still a tear of moisture on her forehead and under her eyes.

"Where d'you come from? England?" he asked.

"Questions?"

"I want to know you."

"Biography? How much?"

"All."

She told him about her parents, father a colonel in the army, mother an inspired amateur gardener, couple of brothers, older, not up to much. A love life that started at fourteen. A fiancé of two years who died in a car crash. Nothing had happened to her—a few cuts and bruises. She became a model, then small parts in movies, then one larger part in a porn movie. Then nothing. Then a high-class escort agency got in touch, and it was very selective, and the guys who took her out took her to good places, and if when they grabbed her at the end of an evening she didn't want to know, then the agency didn't mind if it lost a customer with a flea in his ear. The agency had made the first contract with Almadi two years ago, when the sheikh had visited London. After that the sheikh's social secretary contacted her directly. Four or five times a year she'd fly from London to Brussels, or Rome, or wherever he was doing business. He'd made love to her once. She said he was demanding. But basically he saved screwing for his wives. The rest of the time he just liked pretty naked girls around. He had given her magnificent presents and money. She liked him, but she had witnessed his anger with male associates. She reckoned he was a hard man to do business with.

She talked and Regan listened and smoked. When she finished he said, "Look, there's a chance, remote but possible, that someone's going to try and kill Almadi here. Do something for me. If you go out with him, don't walk near or next to him. Try not to drive in a car with him, don't stay in his bed overnight. We know the work of this assassin, he works close up with an M-38 and he sprays a full clip. Anyone near the victim is likely to catch some of it."

Her expression showed she wasn't taking him too seriously. "I'll survive," she said.

"Napoleon, Wellington, Christ in Jerusalem, they all said that. Take me seriously. Watch out for yourself."

She gave him a bent grin. "I didn't know you cared."

He slowly pushed her back down on the bed. "I'll show you the full extent. . . ."

"The British are changing. I'm a legitimate commentator. I'm fond of your island. I've visited your country each year for the last twenty. It's changed." Sheikh Almadi's steel blue eyes flickered over Regan's face, maybe searching for a line of weakness, but hesitant, as if not finding one. "Years ago, after the war, you were victors living in pauperdom. But princes no less. Now sixty million of you, all lacking confidence, all looking everywhere on the landscape and in your institutions for something to be proud of, finding nothing. A nation that loses its pride loses its confidence, loses the race. I'm sorry for England." The sheikh's eyes had now settled on Regan's.

"England's received lots of obituary notices in its time. The last one from the Germans, 1940."

"The Germans were always mad. The British are not mad. But they are weak. You are supposed to have a democratic system, yet you allow your country to be run by the leaders of the four or five big unions."

"Not quite as simple as that."

The sheikh turned his eyes from Regan to the window, his expression cautious but a little humored. "It is as simple as that. Use a computer or use an abacus. The problem's the same. The answer's the same."

Regan was beginning to get irritated.

"But we're here to talk of something else," the sheikh said gently. "My security. And how we find this man who killed Haffasa."

Regan had entered the Almadi suite at 10:00 A.M., chaperoned by Hijaz and a Bahraini secretary. They had walked from the hall through three reception rooms down a corridor with six bedroom doors and into a sun-room with a massive ebony desk. The normal furniture of the

73

room was wickerwork tables and chaise longues arranged along the west-facing balconies. On the trip through the suite, Regan had seen no girls, and no Jo, whom he'd delivered back to her room at 4:00 A.M.

"There are two ways to handle this. Bring in the French police to surround you with marksmen and bodyguards. The other way is the opposite. To take a risk. To show this man that you aren't surrounded by bevies of bodyguards —that way we would hope to entice him out into the open," Regan said. "That's my idea, but as it's you on the receiving end, you have to make the very difficult decision, sir."

"You appreciate in my country it is normal practice for people like me to wear bullet-proof vests, to be accompanied constantly by bodyguards. But I've always been a kind of exception to this, Mr. Regan," Almadi said. "I've always accepted certain risks and taken them. That's proven by the fact I turned down this man's ransom demand. I could easily have afforded to pay."

"I appreciate that, sir. I've thought about it. I think this is the best way—to convince the man you're a wide-open target. He's a close-up artist. I promise you, he won't reach you before I spot him and stop him."

"You sound very positive, Inspector," Almadi said, and turned to the Bahraini cop. "What does Captain Hijaz think of all this?"

Hijaz was nodding. "Let the man think the task is easy. He will take less precautions. I too expect to be there if he tries to strike."

Almadi was nodding slowly.

"What's your itinerary for today, sir?" Regan asked.

The sheikh told him. Within the hour the French foreign minister would be arriving. He didn't mention the minister's mission. Hijaz had been vague about it at dinner last night. Either the French government was borrowing Bahraini money or Almadi, representing the Bahraini government, was buying something, probably armaments, or Mystère jets.

"The minister comes for an hour. He does not join me for lunch. At one o'clock I shall have my favorite *loup en croûte* at the Vieux Murs."

Hijaz explained where that was. "It's a restaurant on Antibes's seawall, the old town, within walking distance."

"Would you care to walk there, sir?" Regan asked Almadi.

The sheikh mused about the possibilities, then decided. "All right, I will walk. The remainder of the afternoon, rest."

Regan took this to mean girls.

"Eight tonight, light meal at the hotel. Then to Monte Carlo, I meet friends at the Salons Privés. . . ."

"Can you eat at the casino?" Regan asked.

"At the club, yes. Or in the Hôtel du Paris."

"The more public the better."

"We can find a pavement table in the restaurant opposite the Paris. My meal is always just one simple dish."

"Fine," Regan said.

"Arrange that, Captain Hijaz," the sheikh instructed the Bahraini cop.

Hijaz nodded.

Regan caught the slight offhandedness in Hijaz's response. The sheikh was one of the half dozen powerful men of Bahrain, and yet Hijaz was definitely offhanded in dealing with him. Regan made a mental note to investigate that, or simply to find out more about Hijaz and his role with these people.

Almadi was calculating something, studying Regan. "Let me get this clear, Inspector. Are you saying every journey I make from this hotel, you will be accompanying me . . . ?"

Regan nodded. "Yes."

"Ah . . ." Almadi pursed his lips. "Unfortunately, there will be one or two trips to do with quite confidential business between the French government and myself. You will not be able to accompany my party on those assignments."

"Let me make this clear," Regan returned. "I'm either involved in your security or I'm not. If you don't agree with that, I see no reason for remaining any longer here."

Almadi turned and looked at Hijaz for guidance. "He accompanies me all the time?"

Hijaz nodded.

It was the look behind the nod that Regan didn't like. It was hard to interpret it, but somehow easy to guess some of its implications. It was a look that seemed to say, "We can't afford to lose this Yard detective—pay lip service to him. We'll give him the runaround later."

It was a cold, bright afternoon with the breeze prodding the seagulls out of the water to wheel up and head inland. Some round balls of gray cloud started to queue up low on the horizon, readying for a storm.

The fresh breeze had obviously sharpened Almadi's appetite, Jo suggested. After lunch, for dessert, the sheikh had retired with the German redhead, Elke. That left Jo off the hook for a few hours. She'd come to Regan's rooms at 1:30. She'd asked him if he'd had lunch and he'd said no. She said she would take him to lunch at a little restaurant she knew in Antibes town. He said he would take her. She said she knew she made much more money than he. He argued that a Metropolitan policeman was not supposed to live off immoral earnings. She argued that a Metropolitan policeman was de facto living off immoral earnings. Regan put on his overcoat. She covered herself in a floppy wool coat. They left the hotel surreptitiously, but once clear of its acreage held hands as they walked to the port.

Her little restaurant was in the upper square—the awnings flapping and the Pernod umbrellas swaying on street tables. She ordered a salade niçoise and ate most of it with her fingers. He ate little, devoting his attention to how marvelous she looked and how the walk in the sea breeze had freshened the color of her cheeks and, somehow, in untidying her hair had made it even more beautiful.

She asked him about his life, the last few years, his ex-wife, who she was, his seven-year-old daughter, what she was like. He told her, but he didn't make it sound very profound. His history you could find in any cheap paperback. He had really nothing to say about it, except maybe to talk about the mistakes, because sometimes they were interesting. The marriage had been a dead end. His daughter didn't appear to miss him much. Daughter and wife lived with a German bloke, factory manager of a German-owned company in North London. He wished them luck.

"How d'you find your women, Jack?"

"I don't know." He didn't, and he didn't have real answers for her. He was finding she was the kind of woman who asked those simple questions that he in fact had never worked out.

She was watching him dismantle bits of his *croque monsieur*. "Would we work in London, Jack?"

"Work?" He wondered about the definition.

"You know."

He sipped his red wine and filled his eyes with visual images, not mental ones: the awnings flapping in the other two bars in the square, the half dozen housewives bent against the wind, the metal Berliets, humpbacked Deux Chevaux, battered bicycles lining the cobbles, one tasty car, a BMW 2500—but the atmosphere preseason, the town was basically still closed up. In two months from now only one person in three in Antibes would be a native. Meanwhile no grass on the earth patch of the square, and no buds on the trees. Vacant. He felt like that. He didn't know, and yet he did know how to tell her. When both got back to London and met again, it wouldn't work. Because he was older and wiser, and didn't make enough bread, and all the excitement went into his job, and what had killed his marriage had done for every other relationship—the job came first always. Because Regan knew it was his sanity—the elements of force and righteousness and violence within him were answered in the rooms and corridors of Scotland Yard, and in the gray streets and the back alleys of London. He had found in his experience that these were the only elements he could rely on. He had always feared that somehow he was not the whole sum of his parts, but held together by tenuous threads from falling to pieces, falling into a pit of hopelessness, drunkenness, and failure. So he'd made his life a job that occupied twenty-four stressed-up hours a day, and left the slim pickings, the detritus of bits of nights, for his women.

"I like you a great deal, Jo," Regan said. "Back in London we'll see."

They faced the wind and walked back to the hotel along the old seawalls, past the shuttered houses.

He hurried the pace slightly, hoped she wouldn't notice, worried a little, not for himself, but for her safety. There was no question about the identity of the two men in the gray BMW that had followed them on their walk into Antibes at a discreet distance, parked at the opposite side of the square while Regan and Jo ate, and were now following them back to the hotel. He was positive the car contained the two men who had occupied the white Mercedes that had chased the Jag that had tried to kill him in London.

He directed Jo to the main entrance to the hotel. He entered by the rear door, up the steps into reception. He used the house phone.

"Hijaz, I need a car urgently," he said into the phone. "I'm speaking from the front desk."

"What's happened? Why do you say 'urgently'?"

"No time to explain."

"Need any help?"

"No."

"There's a Mercedes 250 SE, hired for general use. Put me on to the head porter. He'll give you the keys."

Regan signaled the head porter over. He handed him the phone.

Half a minute later he walked down the steps and onto the fresh tarmacadam at the back of the hotel. There was only one small Mercedes in the parking lot. He crossed to it, got in and started it, revved the engine, and let it warm for a full two minutes. He anticipated some fast driving, and he didn't want a sluggish engine. He took out the 9mm Walther that Hijaz had given him, thumbed and checked the magazine, pushed it home, then placed it on the seat beside him.

He waited patiently until he saw the needle on the engine temperature gauge start to move. He put the car in gear, headed for the wide gates of the hotel, and nosed out into the Boulevard Kennedy. He turned right, taking the direction back to Antibes town. He had hardly driven fifty yards when he saw the BMW sitting in a little cul-de-sac formed by a driveway leading to a large villa. He drove on and a few seconds later he looked in his driving mirror and saw the gray shape of the other car occupying it.

The route into Antibes town down the Boulevard du Cap is a series of fast straights and sharp corners. He was fifty yards from the Botanical Gardens at the bottom of the wide-laned Boulevard Leclerc when he pulled the auto lever back manually to one, slammed on the brakes, and hurled the car around in a vicious U-turn that nearly had the vehicle over on its roof. The BMW driver's reactions weren't as fast. It bulleted past the Mercedes, and Regan heard the scream of the other car's tires as it slowed down and copied the U-turn.

Regan had achieved his goal. The sudden turn and the close pass to the BMW had given him a perfect close-up of the two men pursuing him. He would know those guys anywhere if he ever saw them again. Neither of them was the man who had killed Haffasa and joined him in the elevator at the Wellington Clinic.

They were now heading back up the peninsula. The shorter of the two men had the gas pedal on the BMW flat to the floor.

Regan saw the passenger in the BMW maneuvering his hand out into slipstream, the glint of sun on the metal of a revolver, a second before the rear window of the Mercedes folded into a thousand particles of glass. The bullet ended up carving a hole into the leather dashboard next to the cigarette lighter. He saw an opening to his left and tapped the steering wheel of the Merc—a little jerk to destabilize the rear wheels and induce the start of a drift. The Merc's rear slued and spun to broadside. Regan gunned the engine, and the car shot off down the side road.

The BMW tried, but didn't make it. It passed the wallowing Mercedes and flew off down the main road, front end down, as the driver slammed on his brakes at ninety miles an hour. Regan got the Merc around the corner but couldn't quite carry the S-bend at the bottom of the lane.

The Merc hit the stone gate of an exclusive villa at around twenty miles an hour. Regan was braced for the crunch and uninjured by it, but the whole front of the car was stoved in, the radiator split, and steam from the overheated engine blew out everywhere. Regan got out and moved around to the other side of the car to open the door and pick up the Walther automatic which had slid off and under the seat with the impact of the collision. He couldn't open the door. The flattening of the front of the Merc must have collapsed the metal door frame sufficiently to jam the passenger door. He started to move back around to the driver's door again.

He saw it—he hadn't heard it. The collision must have taken place at the same time as he was grinding up the metal of the Merc. A pall of black smoke was suddenly rising above the main road a hundred and fifty yards away. The only explanation was that the BMW must have crashed.

If they'd crashed, they wouldn't be in too great shape. It was a risk. But he felt they might be escaping on foot, and he couldn't afford to spend minutes scrabbling around under seats trying to find the Walther.

He ran up the narrow lane and reached the main road. The road surface was black-scarred with the geometry of the Mercedes's drift. He started to walk into the road and halted dead.

Fifty yards away, one of the men was out of the car, gun

in hand. He was the driver, the shorter man. He was pointing it at a startled Frenchman who'd just pulled up in his large Renault alongside the wreck of the BMW. The car's engine was on fire, not a holocaust yet, but the flames were licking along the engine compartment getting stronger. The other BMW occupant lay in the road, writhing and shuddering in agony. Regan made a long-range diagnosis—it looked like the guy had busted his spine. Which gave the shorter man a real problem: how to get the screaming and jerking companion off the road and into the Frenchman's car. Other thoughts would be going through the gunman's mind, like what to do with a dying companion with a broken spine?

The gunman had an answer. Maybe the decision was accelerated by catching a view of Regan a hundred yards away. He fired a shot at Regan. At that range with a pistol it could only be a warning to stay out of range. Then the driver solved his quandary in a brutal way. He went over to his companion and put a bullet in his head.

Regan was staggered by this cold execution under the bright sun. The man who had occupied the passenger seat in the white Mercedes in London and in the gray BMW in Antibes was not going to be telling anyone anything about himself or his friends.

The rest was almost in slow motion. The BMW driver pointed the gun back at the appalled Frenchman and gestured to him to get into his Renault. The BMW driver got in alongside, his revolver still angled at the Frenchman. The Frenchman then did a slow, three-point turn and headed off at a stately speed up the road toward the promontory, leaving the dead man, the car now blazing from stem to stern, and Regan standing there, impotent, in the middle of the road.

Regan speculated as Hijaz tried to get a decision, or a solution, from his own pacing up and down. It had obviously all gone wrong for Hijaz. His face was white with worry and anger. It seemed that most of the anger was about to be directed at Regan.

"Describe them again."

"One of them is still lying up the road two minutes from here. The other I've described."

They were in Hijaz's suite on the third floor. They were alone. Regan wondered about that. Wondered what would happen if the fury that the Bahraini cop was trying to control got out of hand.

"In Allah's name, why did you not recover the Walther before going to see what had happened? You describe how their car was driving very fast. Could you not assume a crash would incapacitate them just long enough for you to find the gun? Events proved this to be the case. If you had done this, Inspector Regan, we would now have both men!" The final sentence ended almost as a shout.

Regan let the man's anger die away for a second. He repeated quietly, "Hijaz, I think you have some idea of who those guys are or were. How can I stay alive long enough to identify the Haffasa killer if you won't even give me the vaguest notion about where the bullets are coming from?"

The fury renewed itself, the color mounting in Hijaz's face. "You are calling me a liar? Are you calling me a liar!?"

Regan saw the indecision in the man's wild eyes. Hijaz was trying to wring the balance between needing Regan for some purpose, some desperate purpose, and wanting to hit him. "Who were they?" Regan asked.

Hijaz exploded in gesticulations. "Who else, you fool! They were part of the team who killed Haffasa. There were three of them. You saw only one that day."

Regan held up a hand to calm and contradict. "The guy in the maroon Jaguar tried to kill me. Not these two. They chased that man in the Jag. They were in pursuit of him. When the Jag smashed me against the wall and I went down on my knees, those men in the Mercedes could have followed through, finished off the job. But they wanted the guy in the Jag. Who are they, Hijaz?"

The temper had gone out of the man as quickly as it had come. He was left glowering at Regan. Regan walked past him, across the room to the balcony. He stood there and looked down at the half dozen official cars that had arrived in the forecourt of the hotel in the last half hour. Hijaz, almost as if on some impulse, came slowly over to the window and joined him, and looked down.

"At the end of this corridor one of the most powerful men in the Arab world is still sitting talking to the French foreign minister. I'm responsible for their security. Those men in the BMW were crucial to this security problem. You can see, then, why I am disappointed in your actions. . . ."

Regan himself had arrived at a verdict and decided that Hijaz should have it. "I'm going to fall back a bit—keep my distance. The fact is I don't trust you or your friends anymore. I'll go through the motions. Every time Sheikh Almadi leaves the hotel, I'll be there. But I'll be making certain new arrangements for myself."

"Like what?" Hijaz asked sharply.

"I'll probably be moving out of this hotel. You see, we mustn't forget a key element in this business. I saw a killer. I have to protect myself. From now on I'll operate separately."

"Your second mad mistake in one day," Hijaz said softly, then drank down the rest of his scotch.

"It's an interesting performance," Regan thought, "well done but still one hundred percent phony. Not only the sentiments, but the man." Regan felt sure that Hijaz knew the identity of the two in the BMW. Anybody else would have rushed out there to study the face of the corpse lying with a bullet in its brain. But Hijaz hadn't. That begged a sizable question. There were a hundred answers, but the one that would be head and shoulders above the rest in Regan's mind was the simplest one. Could it be that Hijaz's job, far from protecting one of the most important men in the Arab world, might be the opposite, finding the appropriate occasion to put assassin and the sheikh together?

He was uncertain of the French CID's investigation procedures in dealing with a man with a bullet hole in his head on the Boulevard du Cap, Antibes. There was a series of huddles in the hotel, first Almadi and the French foreign minister, who just happened to still be with him when the man was being shot. They, on the minister's advice, both talked to the local CID chief of the Nice prefecture, a tall man named Guignard with light gray hair and bootblack eyebrows. The foreign minister in the presence of Guignard phoned the Justice Ministry in Paris and found a bigwig to talk to Guignard and order him not to bother Almadi or his entourage under any circumstances, but to supply any information to the sheikh that he required. The next huddle involved Guignard, Hijaz, and the sheikh. The third huddle involved Regan, Guignard, and Hijaz. By now the time was four-thirty in the afternoon. Outside, the world was turning colder and grayer. Inside, Regan was getting tired of hotel corridors and rooms and waiting for results of meetings. At four-thirty precisely the local prefecture received the news that the murderer had gotten the unwilling Renault owner to ferry him along the coast, up the N7, and to Marseille. Regan reckoned on that particular route they must have passed at least a hundred French cops, each furnished with a description of the wanted car, either sprawled on their motorcycles or lounging on corners picking the remnants of garlic cloves out of their teeth. The news supplied by the owner of the Renault, who'd raced into a police station in a suburb of Marseille, took exactly forty minutes to percolate through the French police and phone systems to Guignard pacing in the lobby of the Hôtel du Cap. Guignard went into a tirade. He had two junior detectives with him. As he had no one else to shout at, he shouted at them.

Regan thought Guignard a bright guy. He had moved his end fast. The guy shot dead by the burning BMW had, it turned out, no papers on him, no labels in his clothes. Guignard had the dead man's clothes driven high speed into Nice, which conveniently had a small forensic laboratory in the police headquarters in Rue de France. They ripped the clothes to pieces. The man's shoes had been Italian, Gucci, obtainable in any capital city in the Western world. But when the label-less jacket was cut apart with scissors, the stiffening canvas material inside the collar had a strip of small stencil markings on the canvas. The markings simply repeated *W3*. The prefecture at Nice called Paris Central Police Headquarters, who keep a register of French clothing trademarks and laundry marks. The marking *W3* was not known. Without reference back, Paris HQ contacted Scotland Yard, who also keep lists of clothing trademarks and laundry marks. *W* stood for "Willerby," an English multiple clothing store manufacturing men's suitings; *3* stood for the third quality of canvas used as a collar liner.

This news came, via Guignard, to Regan at 5:00 P.M. Regan was pleased to hear it. Any information that suggested that the two men, first inhabiting the Merc in London, then the BMW in Antibes, anything that showed they had a connection to England was good news. It suggested that eventually he'd identify a London end to the investigation. There had always been the problem in the Haffasa case that the killing had involved people, and issues, that had absolutely nothing to do with the United Kingdom. It was likely he'd been wasting his time investigating people who would be found to be at loose in the world at large.

At 6:15 Regan met the French foreign minister. The top politico had again met with Almadi, then gone away to confer with some colleagues on the end of a telephone, then come back for another meeting with the sheikh. Almadi meanwhile had called Regan in to hear his version of the incident.

Regan told the story to Almadi simply and without embroidery. The sheikh had echoed Hijaz's words. "A tragedy you did not recover the Walther automatic before you ran to the main road."

Regan shrugged. "There are an increasing number of regrettable elements in this case."

"What are you saying?" Almadi asked, his eyelids lowering a fraction, making his face even more of a mask.

"I've concluded that the feedback from you people," Regan turned to defer the accusation in the direction of Hijaz, "is often lies. I don't believe in the blackmailer killing King Faisal. I don't believe your life is being threatened for money."

Hijaz had said nothing. Almadi's face remained expressionless for a long moment. Then he said, "Perhaps you're right."

"Well, I'd like a complete story, and no lies."

Almadi pondered that, almost as if he was playing blackjack at the Monaco casino and the decision was to turn a card, or stick.

Regan listened to the gravel of the man's deep voice clearing itself, and the sheikh spoke.

"You're perceptive, Mr. Regan. Yes indeed, the truth is you haven't been told the truth. You may reject us and return to London. Alternatively, if you will postpone your questioning for a few more hours, I promise then you will be told everything. Obviously I need you because you are the man who saw the assassin. The fact is I cannot tell you the whole truth for perhaps twenty-four hours. The choice is

Regan gave it a slow once-over in his mind. There was no decision—twenty-four hours was neither here nor there. "Okay, I'll give you a day. Then Hijaz will tell me who those men in the BMW were."

"You think we know?" Almadi looked first at Regan, and then at Hijaz.

"I know he knows," Regan said. But he suddenly had the uncomfortable feeling that part of his calculations might be wrong—this new assumption was that Almadi and Hijaz were equal parties as liars. Now maybe not; maybe Hijaz was on his own. Maybe Almadi was ignorant of everything, ignorant and totally in Hijaz's untrustworthy care.

It was at this point that the secretary entered and spoke to Almadi in Arabic.

Hijaz translated. "The foreign minister has returned. We will now leave, Inspector Regan."

"Stay." Almadi said it sharply, with a look to Hijaz that might be some kind of warning to the Bahraini cop to remember who gave the orders.

90

The minister, Monsieur de Laubenque, was a dapper man, light-blue suited, with matching blue eyes that looked down for two reasons. First, because he was tall, and second, because he was the possessor of a personality that looked down on people.

Almadi rose from behind the solarium desk and crossed to the tall man, shook his hand for what must have been the second or third time this day. Almadi indicated Regan and introduced him. "From Scotland Yard, Inspector Regan. The man who has seen the enemy who murdered bin Haffasa."

That struck a note with Regan—why had Almadi mentioned his name previously to de Laubenque—an innocuous conversation, or something else?

"I hope you are getting all the cooperation you need from the Nice prefecture," de Laubenque said, looking down at Regan. The man's English was faultless. "I regret the incident here in Antibes this afternoon, but I believe the clothing now identifies one of the persons as probably English."

"Possibly," Regan said.

De Laubenque looked sour. "I said probably, Inspector. I hope you will prevent Englishmen or anybody else from any further incidents during our honored guest's visit."

Almadi decided the conversation had reached a conclusion. "I will be going to the restaurant, the Oasis, at La Napoule—at eight o'clock tonight—a brief meal. I trust you will accompany my party," he said to Regan.

"I'll be among your escort."

"Then I will see you later, Inspector," Almadi said. Regan nodded, and then nodded to the French minister, turned and walked to the door of the solarium and out. As he walked down the corridors and out of the suite, he could hear Hijaz's soft footsteps on the carpet behind him. But he didn't look back. He took the elevator down one floor to his room.

It was to turn out to be a depressing evening. Four cars made the trip from Antibes along the coast road the forty kilometers to La Napoule. Hijaz with a chauffeur in the first car, Almadi and two of the girls in the second, a Mercedes 280 SEC, then Regan and a chauffeur in a third car, and then a social secretary and a couple of French civil servants in a fourth Mercedes.

Regan's depression was filed under two categories. First, the coast roads were heavily trafficked. Every half-collapsed Deux Chevaux and pensioned-off Citroen were behaving like Ferraris. The hit-and-run approach of these cars down the side of the stately cortege of Mercedeses would resemble the sort of approach that the BMW killer would make. Second, the Oasis Restaurant was half full and taking bookings at the door. Regan had assumed that any restaurant Almadi and company would choose would at least have an elementary security screen in only accepting phone bookings. But people were wandering in and out of the place like a public toilet. As he sat outside the restaurant, he could see that any guy with a gun would have little trouble getting past himself and Hijaz if he was determined to make an attempt on Almadi.

Regan had stationed himself alone in his car outside the

restaurant. The Oasis was spread out behind a high wall with a wide porticoed entrance leading into a cobbled courtyard. There was floodlighting down from trees on the yard, which had an ornamental fountain. The main restaurant lay behind sheets of plate glass so guests could overlook the cobbles and the fountain. Almadi's party couldn't have made better targets if they had been individually stood under a spotlight. Regan decided on a car-bound seat outside, covering the entrance. Hijaz was at a table just inside the front foyer. Almadi and his French guests and the two girls had a window seat. One was the German girl, Elke; the other was Jo.

She was looking more beautiful than ever. The dress blue, silky, diaphanous, falling as lightly around the curves of her figure as her laughter—he could hear her laughter through the open restaurant doors. There was nothing fake there; she was enjoying herself. The French civil servants spent the two hours offering as much to her and her needs as to Almadi—and when they were not singling her out for their probes of witticism, Almadi was talking to her, carefully, earnestly, as if they were almost husband and wife, this member of the world's super-rich caring for her, studying her needs, snapping his fingers for more attention for her from the waiters. She was in her element, and Regan watched it, the performance, and wondered about the quality of his own madness— that he had thought that he could compete here, a burnt-out London cop so punch-drunk with his collisions with life that he had nothing to offer her, especially not his future.

She had managed earlier, in the foyer of the Hôtel du Cap, while the Mercs were arriving and circling, to give him a millisecond's conspiratorial look, a miniature communication that said, "Hi, Jack Regan, forgive me while I go through all this shit—a girl's got to make a living. And please don't let these guys guess about you and me. . . ." Or had she? Had that actually been the message of that look? Or was its brevity a simple message? How many guys, at a conservative guess, would he think she had slept with in the last Gregorian calendar year—a hundred? A cop's got to be a fun experience to be noted in grafitti on the chalk cliffs of her experience. Yes, she'd said, "Would it work back in London for us, Jack?" But what in hell did that mean?

Jack Regan sat out his vigil in the car, watching Almadi, a man who could probably buy London, probably would, treating her with the reverence of a queen. His speculations passed into query and crisis—at the end of two hours he thought about it, searched his memory, but he couldn't remember any other time in his life when he'd felt more depressed about a girl.

The N204 Nice to Cuneo is more a switchback than a road, and sections of it have been used to separate the boys from the men in the last hours of the Monte Carlo Rallye, some of the boys landing up on the bottom of the myriad of chasms and ravines. The road to Cuneo seems to have been designed with the idea of preventing anyone getting to this no-man's-land town between Nice and Turin. Of course there's the autostrada, which makes the Monaco-Turin hop a shopping trip—but it's the old road, of deep crevasses, gaunt mountains, and tinkling waterfalls streaking silver among the pines that Almadi's party took the next morning in four Mercedeses.

Hijaz rode as usual in front, chauffeur driven in a black Mercedes 220. Sheikh Almadi rode in the second car— three French officials with him and the chauffeur, so it was a tight fit for everyone inside that Mercedes. Regan rode alone in the back of the third Merc. He too had a Hertz chauffeur who spoke English and had traveled everywhere and said he had his shirts tailored in London, and talked about all the important people he knew and after half an hour of this had bored Regan stiff. In the fourth car, a chauffeur and two more French officials.

Hijaz had told him, like a nanny carefully explaining the details of an outing to a child, that they were going to a French factory plant near Tende, just this side of the Italian border. Sheikh Almadi was to inspect some installations. For Regan's information these installations were guarded by military personnel. So the only security problems involved the journey there and back.

Regan had nodded. Regan didn't care too much. He'd just had a night's sleep on the problems of yesterday and found some of them were not resolvable. Like Hijaz knew a lot about the people in the BMW and was not telling Regan. Well, that wasn't good enough. But he wasn't about to start a tendentious row. He'd decided he'd call the Yard at 5:30 tonight, just when Maynon would have left the building, but while DCI Haskins was still there. He would tell Haskins he was pissed off and coming home. Hijaz had said in the nanny speech there was a possibility that Almadi, if the morning's trip went well, might pull out tomorrow, heading back for Bahrain. There were, de facto, a priori, and phrases from other dead lingos, things that Regan would not do, lengths to which he would not go, calls beyond acceptable duties. It was as simple as that—he was not of a mind to accompany Almadi back to the khaki deserts, flyswatter in one hand and binoculars in the other, searching forever the burning dunes for the thin-faced assassin of the Wellington Clinic. Sod the lot, he was off. He had not told Hijaz yet.

He sat in the Merc on the road to Cuneo—the only concession to his job the blue steel, blunt-nosed 9mm Walther, the gun which he'd unhappily left in the car before the Antibes killing. He felt pessimistic about everything. His face was sour, his eyes mild angered. The road kept torturing itself around, trying to find a way up the valleys. The cars kept crossing low bridges over rushing rivers filled with wood and brush torn by the torrent, and little valleys of greensward where maybe in ages past Roman mobs in centurion gear had kipped the night prior to a move west to lean on some Gauls. Regan remembered Caesar's Commentaries—that's what the wops used to do for a laugh. They'd spent two centuries kicking the shit out of the southern frogs, just for some *herbes de Provence* in their pasta.

His mind ranged, touching on thoughts provoked and soured by the gaunt scenery, as the four Mercedeses made their stately climb upward through the valleys. Jo had affected him. What a dumb-assed thing to happen. Soft blue eyes, and a penchant for a screw with a check at the end of it. Right? Wrong. Who was he to fall for her? Who was he to fall for anyone? Didn't he know himself? Hadn't he evolved, some years after the bust-up of the matrimonial home, a studied system of rapid rutting with some nonaligned broad and at the precise moment when it might change gear, as it always did, a quick burial ceremony with the excuse of a lot of work? Exit girlfriend. No, he'd tried all that permanence, living together, joint bank accounts. He had actually intended his marriage to work and had been quite shocked when it didn't, when she left him. She, who didn't have the energy to raise her eyes for a loan, had got the whole bastard thing together inside twenty-four hours and said farewell to Jack Regan—she hadn't brought it up before, but it was all quite decided that this was good-bye time. That was unfair, he decided, as he looked out over the valleys. The problem with the marriage was he didn't think there was a problem until it was too late. Eight billion marriages a year go down in the same flames. The pine trees nodded their heads at him, either in complete agreement or because of the upwind from the gorges.

Jo was an entirely beautiful girl, from sex to simple conversation. But the thing that screwed him here was that he'd never met a bird before, not one, that he'd thought was too good for him. Well, he'd met his match in a bedroom in the Hôtel du Cap. That was the lousiest discovery he'd ever made in his life. There were a thousand ice-cold handsome millionaires in the world who would turn in a couple of shipping fleets to grab that ass. He had watched those guys last night, the simian French civil servants and Almadi, flutter around her, moths to the flame. He felt like lifting up the Walther, telling the Hertz chauffeur to overtake the Almadi car, and shooting some neat holes in Almadi's head—a symbolic blow for the little people of the world. But he wouldn't do it, because the one thing about Jo that he was sure of was that he had already lost

The line of Mercedeses had now come out onto a high, wide plateau, low foothills still to the right of the road. The lead car slowed. Regan gave up his gloom. He'd be back in London tonight. He'd remembered a bird he knew, met her six months ago on a pub raid in Harmonsworth. He'd given it to her twice, once on her birthday— her nicest present, she'd said. Not a bad-looking kid and as hot as a raw pepper. He'd go there tonight. He'd take a bottle of Bell's and bury himself in that lot. He would forget sitting outside that restaurant, the Oasis in La Napoule, last night, watching Jo and loving her.

The lead Mercedes took a left turn off the main road and up a tarmacadam road into a new valley sheer with rocks. The three cars followed.

Half a kilometer up the valley, the first fresh-paint, steel signs. ATTENTION A 100 METRES, PRIVEE. ATTENTION. PROPRIETE PRIVEE. GOUVERNEMENT DE FRANCE. A hundred meters on, the first car halted. A metal fence blocked the road. In the fence a wide high set of steel gates. On each side of the gates high steel trellis towers with floodlights. By the left-hand gate, a low shed, looking like the guardroom of a regimental building. Standing around the shed were four uniformed soldiers, each with a submachine gun. Two of the soldiers were near the closed gates. It was evident that the procession of Mercedeses had been expected. An officer, also armed, came smartly out of the hut at the appearance of the first Mercedes and signaled the two guards on the gate to open it wide. The four Mercedeses drove through.

For the last five minutes on the main road there had been little sign of humanity, but once inside the gates, and on the further half-kilometer drive up to the main installations, Regan surveyed a hive of activity. Workmen, soldiers, earth-moving equipment, cranes, trucks, a helicopter sitting on a clearing among pine trees, forklift trucks passing with building materials, the large site crisscrossed with recently made cement roads. At the end of the main approach road a group of around a dozen buildings.

Four of the buildings were large enough to be aircraft hangars. But Regan saw that each contained suites of offices, and car parks. Something about the whole place struck him as curious. There must be hundreds of people in the vicinity of this complex, but they'd passed no cars or any other traffic on the road up to the main gates of the installation. Obviously it was a self-contained community. It looked like a dozen things. It could've been an airport, but it didn't have any runways. It looked like an astronomical observatory; two of the buildings had huge, half-spherical metal roofs, with open panels in them.

Regan's chauffeur halted the car. Regan picked up the Walther, pocketed it, and climbed out. Almadi and the three French civil servants were already out of the larger Mercedes and heading now, deep in conversation, toward a low building which looked like a reception center.

Regan took a quick look around. Again, many people in the vicinity, many vantage points for a potential assassin. But he could see a couple of armed soldiers, one a captain, stepping out from another low building and moving over toward the cars. Evidently security had been organized inside the complex.

He started to move off after Almadi and the three Frenchmen. Hijaz stepped out from behind the first parked Mercedes and intercepted him.

"It will not be necessary to accompany Sheikh Almadi on his tour of these buildings," Hijaz said. "In fact he insists that neither you nor I accompany him."

Regan shrugged. "Suit yourself. What is this complex? I notice it doesn't advertise itself."

"It's a government installation," Hijaz stated.

"That's obvious to a child. What kind of installation?"

"Just a French government complex."

Regan looked hard at Hijaz. "D'you ever answer a straight question?"

Hijaz didn't seem to care. "The answer is implicit—the answer is, don't ask questions. . . ."

"I'm leaving for England tonight," Regan said suddenly, the voice unaggressive, just tired. "I can't respond to people like you. I don't think I give a damn anymore whether anybody puts a bullet in any one of you."

It was as if Hijaz had a piece of food in his mouth and was chewing it over. "I don't think it matters if you go. Sheikh Almadi signs the deal with the French this afternoon. We had to protect him to the point where he signed that deal. . . ."

"What deal?"

Hijaz shook his head. "In a way I'm sorry for you. You've never understood anything about anything. You never will."

Regan wasn't going to rise to it. He went back and sat in the car. Hijaz strolled off toward the reception building.

Almadi was there an hour and a quarter. From time to time Regan, either sitting inside the Merc or stretching his feet in a tour of the perimeter of the car park, saw the sheikh with his escort coming out of one building and heading into another. The sheikh's escort now numbered about a dozen people. The original three senior civil servants who had traveled in his car and the two who had traveled in the fourth Merc were now joined by another half dozen men all in laboratory technicians' white coats.

At five minutes after midday, Almadi, surrounded now by at least a dozen white-coated technicians in addition to the dark-suited civil servants, arrived back in the car park. With much bowing and handshaking on the part of everyone present, he got into the car. Hijaz walked down from the first Mercedes and poked his head into Regan's car. "We'll take a different route back. A normal precaution. All right?"

"All right," Regan said. He had just found out that his Hertz chauffeur who'd traveled everywhere and got his shirts tailored in London had in fact been quietly slavering his way through a copy of the magazine *Oui*, which he'd placed in the mid-pages of his *Le Monde*.

Regan signaled him as he put *Le Monde* aside to start the car that he, Regan, had spotted the flesh acres and would appreciate a view. Wordlessly the chauffeur handed over the magazine.

Regan opened the mag. The four Mercedeses moved into U-turns and headed off down the road to the steel gates.

The handshaking was now replaced by waves from the white-coated men they were leaving behind. Regan didn't join in. He sat back and studied the centerfold of a sixteen-year-old who was put together in such a way that, from the simple forensic evidence contained in the photo of the body, Regan knew men were going to kill each other or themselves in desperate effort for possession.

There wasn't a lot that could be done to vary the route from Tende. They took a half-made lane to Sorres which eventually led to the Grande Corniche.

Regan looked up from *Oui* at Eze-La Turbie. They were in the center of the village. There was a Friday morning market on in a square which, according to the parking signs, was normally a car park. A Peugeot bread van had just pulled up alongside the Merc. The man driving the van had a mustache. Suddenly Regan was sure of two things. The mustache was a new one, and the driver of the bread van was the killer who had accompanied him down in the elevator of the Wellington Clinic.

Regan lifted the copy of *Oui* up another couple of inches to completely hide his face. But he felt sure the man had not spotted him. The freshly mustached killer's attention was riveted on the Mercedes in front, and what could be seen through its rear window—the back of the slate-gray head of Almadi seated to the right of one of the French officials.

Slowly Regan's hand moved inside and under the left lapel of his jacket, found the butt of the Walther, and eased it out of the shoulder holster.

The traffic lights that had held up the cortege changed to green, but there was still an uncertain milling around of housewives and stall-holders crossing the road, and the stream of traffic took a few more seconds to get under way.

Meanwhile the bread van nipped in between Almadi's Mercedes and Regan.

Regan dropped the copy of *Oui*, leaned forward, spoke to the chauffeur, and pulled out all the stops on a performance that would have had Sir John Gielgud checking back over his career to see where he had gone wrong. "This is Eze, isn't it? I was here a few days ago. Could you do me a great favor? That tobacconist over there," he pointed to a tobacconist on the other side of the square, "sells British cigarettes called Embassy. I came here to Les Hauts. I bought some Embassy. I think he shortchanged me. Ten francs he charged for two packs."

103

"Ten francs, two packs? You were robbed."

"Well, that's what I thought. You couldn't possibly do me a favor and get some more Embassy for me at the right price?" Regan stuffed a ten-franc note into the top pocket of the chauffeur's jacket.

"Okay," the chauffeur said. "I'll be a second."

He got out of the car and signaled the fourth Mercedes in the line to overtake and follow off after Hijaz's and Almadi's cars and the bread van.

The chauffeur crossed the square and entered the tobacconist. Regan almost fell out of the rear door in his haste to get into the front behind the driver's wheel. But once installed he took another couple of seconds to put on the chauffeur's hat and the dark driving glasses which the man had left behind. The Hertz chauffeur had switched the engine off. Regan turned the key in the ignition, slammed the accelerator pedal to the floor, and took off with a couple of black Pirelli signatures marking his exit from the square.

He could almost physically smell the danger. It was as if he knew that death, not his death, but Almadi's, was probably seconds away, and yet before he could act, he must think, use his God-given intelligence to sort out a precise organization of thoughts to translate into action. He'd gotten a car—he'd had to take it away from the Hertz chauffeur because he intended to risk the auto, wreck it if necessary, use it as a battering ram, whatever. There would have been no time to explain that or any part of it to the chauffeur. And the man would have said no anyhow—it was not part of his job to smash up his employer's assets.

Regan cut through the traffic which had meanwhile lined up behind the Hijaz and Almadi Mercs, closely followed by the bread van and the other Merc. The road was falling and narrowing down now toward Nice and the Baie des Anges, glimpses of the sea below among the cotton clouds that were drifting, at this height, through the precipices of the high road. His first decision was to find a precise spot in the oncoming series of S-bends seesawing down the sides of the gorges, a hundred-yard stretch in which to attempt to overtake three cars and the bread van. That was phase number one. Phase number two, which Regan was now rapidly drafting as the only phase-two possibility, was difficult to contemplate. He had to stop the bread van—but not by killing the driver. He must stop the driver in what looked like a genuine accident, because he had phase number three to think about. He wanted the killer of the Wellington Clinic walking away from the bread van. He wanted that man intact, leading him back to the people who gave him his orders. The only thing that Regan really wanted to sort out in this whole glad bag of crime was who in hell employed the man with the false mustache to blow the holes in Haffasa in the Wellington Clinic, London, England.

That was Regan's case—to solve and answer that. Nothing else. That's what the British taxpayer wanted in return for his wages. And the first step on the route to that would be near suicide.

He saw the opening. He kicked the accelerator to the floor and pulled the car out of the downhill traffic in a scream of rear tires. There were two cars in front of him, then the tail Mercedes, then the bread van. Even the French drivers with their national weakness for road slaughter reacted immediately in a cacophony of horns as Regan sliced down their left-hand sides in a desperate attempt to reclaim a position by the time he reached the first blind corner.

Somehow he did it, but there was no good reason for it. The Mercedes 200 was not a performance car. He made it on luck and brakes. He slued the heavy car sideways around the S-bend and reviewed the new situation. There was now one car, a Peugeot, in front of him, and in front of the Peugeot, the Mercedes and the bread van.

He banged on the accelerator again and hauled the car out on the wrong side of the road. He was now on a straight about a hundred and fifty yards long, with a sign halfway down it which he could already see, forecasting a double S-bend at the bottom. There was a lorry lumbering up toward him. He could almost see the driver's face go white as blood and lunchtime Pernod drained out of it. He could hear a shouted blasphemy from the Peugeot driver, a large, bald-headed man, as he pulled the Merc with an inch to spare past the Peugeot, out past the Merc, in for a second into the gap behind the bread van, and then, risking everything, pulled the car out again, overtook the bread van, angling his face away from its driver. But the latter would have enough on his mind holding on to his piece of road as Regan sliced past him, just missing the lorry coming uphill, which by now had thrown on its brakes to avoid a head-on collision.

He was now between Almadi's car and the van. Now

phase three. He had to stop the bread van without killing himself or its driver.

He studied the killer in the interior mirror. He had no worries that the killer would recognize him—all he was presenting to the killer's eyes was the back of a head with a chauffeur's hat on it.

He began to close in on the rear of the Almadi car. The chauffeur in the Almadi car automatically increased the speed with the result that the two started to bunch up with the Hijaz Mercedes in the lead. Hijaz's driver increased his speed.

They were still trailing downhill, down from the giddy heights of the Grande Corniche, toward the coast. The three leading Mercs nudging each other, picking up speed. The speed reached and passed the seventy mark. The old Peugeot bread van behind started to fall back. The killer had calculated the risks and decided to come down on the side of caution. Or maybe there were other reasons—the brakes might not be up to it if this downhill chase had to come to a sudden halt. Or maybe the killer knew precisely where they were heading, had known Almadi's residence was the Hôtel du Cap since Almadi's arrival, or even before.

The bread van began to lose ground. Regan searched for the moment, looked for the suitable lay of the land where he could play his hand. The road wandering down through the *massif* was still narrow; only on stretches did it run to two wide lanes where it was possible to overtake. Now, ahead, another warning of a double S-bend as the road snaked around the extremities of two abutting cliffs.

Regan knew, even before he'd gotten around the bend and explored the topography, that the time was now. The bread van was a hundred yards behind him as he accelerated the Mercedes around the bend, positioned the car dead center of the road, and threw on the brakes. The Merc burned itself to a smoking-rubber halt. Regan sat there, stiff as a statue, keyed to a millisecond's reaction as he studied the rear mirror. The bread van was about to come around the blind corner and hit him square in the rear. Regan powered up to the maximum revs, the engine screaming and the car shaking.

The bread van was suddenly careening around the corner and coming at the rear of Regan's car full tilt. Regan hesitated a split second. That second was to give the killer time to work it out. The killer had three choices, to steer to the left and end up hitting the low wall and sailing in his bread van over the precipice, to steer dead center and hit Regan's car square in the rear and end up with his body impaled in the mess of twisted metal of the bread van's front and the Merc's rear, or—the only other possibility—to drive the van into the deep storm ditch to the right of the road. That was the choice Regan wanted him to make. That was the choice he made.

The storm ditch was six feet wide, four feet deep, and walled in on the right by the vertical rock face. The bread van hit the ditch as Regan hit the accelerator. While Regan in the Merc was haring off down the road, the bread van was ripping itself to pieces in its journey along the ditch. Regan saw one of the van's front tires split and spin off up into the air. But he knew the killer would step out of the sixty-mile-an-hour crash intact. His object was achieved.

He caught up with the Almadi Mercedes and tailed it through the switchback of the second S-bend. Immediately beyond this, a turning off the Grande Corniche led presumably down to the Moyenne Corniche. Regan took the left turn as the other two Mercedeses sailed on down the Grande Corniche heading for Nice.

He drove down the tree-lined tarmacadam tributary of the main road, huge luxury villas behind high walls on each side. He drove a hundred yards, halted, did a three-point turn, and headed back up and turned right again, pointing the car upward toward the scene of the bread van crash.

He had noticed a garage with an AUTO LAVAGE sign about three hundred yards down from the scene of the crash. It was on the left-hand side of the road. He was taking a certain risk, but he drove the car fast up and turned into the garage. He'd also noticed the garage had a FERME sign in its forecourt; the pump attendants were probably off to lunch. He drove the car around to the back of the garage and into the empty tunnel of the nonfunctioning car wash. He got out, threw the chauffeur's cap and dark glasses inside, locked the car, and then started off for the stiff walk up to the second of the S-bends. The bread van had crashed around the corner from the first of the S-bends. Regan approached the corner carefully. There were some bushes growing out of the ditch at the side of the road, and he moved in among them. He could see the little scenario without being seen. A couple of motorists had stopped to assist the killer. Their two cars were parked haphazardly on the road and were causing a backup of traffic. The killer was standing upright, looking shaken but obviously not damaged. He was gesticulating with the matching gesticulations of the other two, presumably describing a certain chauffeur's insane driving and how it had ended him up in a ditch.

Then Regan was suddenly running downhill back to the deserted garage, because he'd seen the killer pointing at his watch, and the Peugeot owner agreeing and gesturing him toward the Peugeot. The killer was obviously talking about his need to get somewhere on time and requesting a lift. And the Peugeot owner was consenting. The two men were heading for the Peugeot.

Regan covered the three hundred yards to the garage in record time. He had hardly run inside the car wash and halted to look back up the road when he saw the gray Peugeot, now with its two occupants, appear and disappear down the road toward Nice. Regan got into the car, fumbled with the ignition key, got it started. He put it in reverse and shot out of the car wash. Seconds later he was back on the Grande Corniche. Thirty seconds later he was tucked in behind a small Alfa Romeo sports car which was trailing a Porsche, which was sitting on the tail of the Peugeot. Cautiously Regan navigated the last five miles of the journey into Nice.

The Grande Corniche enters the north of Nice down the Boulevard Risso, which runs into the Esplanade General de Gaulle. The Peugeot pulled over by the cab rank in the long square. The man with the mustache got out, a cursory wave to the bald head in the Peugeot, and the killer walked over and talked to a cabman, then climbed into his cab. Regan had braked a hundred yards back from the switch of vehicles. He now filtered off slowly as the cab, with the killer inside, headed down the east side of the square for the port.

Regan saw the sea, and out in the bay the white horses of the cold, unsettled water. The breeze pulled at raincoats on the brave strollers on the front, and fluttered the awnings of the empty pavement bars. He was sure the cab was going to take a right along the Promenade des Anglais and find the route out past the airport, Cap 3000, and south to Antibes. He was sure his luck was out, his calculations too optimistic. He wanted the M-38 expert to head him to base. Now he felt that all the guy was going to do was to return to the Almadi tail—that had been the man's objective when he'd picked up the sheikh's party at the secret installation. He'd lost his bread van, but now that he had a new set of wheels, why should he change objectives? It all seemed obvious and logical. Regan almost did a double take when the cab made a left at the bottom of the Jardin Albert Premier. The killer's destination was east. He was heading in the opposite direction from Antibes.

Regan trailed the car carefully. The killer would be shaken, suspicious. The cab had to make the journey down the side of the old port and right, across the top of it. The killer only had to incline his head slightly at the north end of the port to see Regan's Mercedes. But he obviously had other things on his mind and didn't look back.

Regan saw a sign: CORNICHE INFERIOR; VILLEFRANCHE; BEAULIEU. The cab accelerated up and through the mild mess of lunchtime motorists and cyclists seeking meals away from the expense of the town proper. Regan earned one waved fist and a horn quartet from another outraged group as he cut and thrust with the Mercedes to keep the cab in view and at a distance of no more than a hundred yards between himself and his quarry.

The road to Beaulieu was a repetition of the pendulum route of the Grande Corniche, save this time the ascents and descents were mild. Regan passed pink villas, perched on the rock, imported direct from Disneyland, and low castles behind lawns bordered by private driveways, each pebble hand selected and polished by Cartier. He passed million-dollar houses lined up like the ribbon development of a fast-buck builder, but he hardly noticed them because his eyes were on the cab, and his brain on his calculations.

Where was the killer going? Where else but some kind of base, house, apartment. Maybe a boat? Below the walls of the coast, down in the gullies of little ports and *plages* made by man, a continuing spawn of marinas, hundreds and hundreds of fiberglass dreams from ninety feet to nine, from oceangoing cruisers to tiny sailboats, sails up, scattered through the harbors and out on the surface of the ocean like confetti at a wet wedding. Maybe a plane? Maybe the guy was heading for a private plane or helicopter. There were bound to be small private airports or heliports along this coastline, certain to be one in Monaco. Now that might be something that Regan would

112

not be able to handle. That's what worried him almost as much as the need to keep the cab in sight, not lose it for one second. What worried Regan was that it wasn't enough for him or anybody else just to arrest this man. That would solve no problems, give no answers. He had the killer. The man might escape. But he was after more than this gent who'd dispatched Haffasa in the Wellington Clinic, he was after the reason for it. It was just a gamble that the man, if allowed his head for a few more hours, would lead him to the answers. Regan had never turned down a gamble in his life.

The villa lay low and sprawled down the south side of the first small western promontory on Cap Ferrat. There was a white-sprayed wall ten feet high all around the perimeter of its unseen gardens. It looked like a wall, but maybe it was a fortification; maybe it was designed to resist armor-piercing shells or heavy mortar attack. The house had a set of double steel gates with a large man hanging around inside the gates. The man had on a dark blue suit and presumably served the same purposes as a Doberman pinscher—he was there to eat anyone who thought it might be fun to call. Regan nosed the Merc gently over the railway bridge to glide onto the peninsula of St. Jean Cap Ferrat, pulling further back from the cab as he saw the universal cul-de-sac sign on a street post. This cul-de-sac was obviously the end of the ride.

Regan saw the cab pull in and halt. The guy got out and

paid the driver, who sat there a minute checking the francs away into various change pockets in his paunch. Regan spotted the huge man inside of the gates move a lot quicker than a man of his size was expected to, open the gates, and allow the Wellington Clinic killer to.enter. Not a word was exhanged between guard and killer. They knew each other. Regan eased the Merc back five yards up the lane, around a first slight bend, and halted. He got out.

Meanwhile the cab had turned around, produced a dust cloud on the private road, and headed up past Regan. Regan was a little unsure of his next move. The ten-foot-high villa wall effectively screened from view the whole ground and first floor of the three-floor villa. He must find some crow's nest in the hills and hollows of this mogul's two-mile strip of real estate to get a view down and over the walls into the white villa.

He got back into the car, turned it around, and drove up the quarter-mile lane to the railway bridge and then took the left turn off the peninsula. He retraced the road a quarter-mile west, in the Villefranche direction, parked and got out of the car, and crossed to the road wall. The Villefranche coast road at this point was stuck on a cliff five hundred feet above sea level. Regan had stopped at a point where the germane parts of the white villa could quite easily be seen. The first and second floors were revealed through a clearing in the small woods of palm and acacia which screened most of that part of the promontory.

He saw several men. He started to count and got to six.

They were on an open veranda at the sea end of the ground floor. The veranda in fact was cantilevered out over a large, kidney-shaped swimming pool. The men all seemed to be large like the gateman, and they also wore dark suits. The killer was among them. Regan could recognize him over the distance of five hundred yards. He was the only one with a mustache on his face. The men were talking animatedly out under the sun on the veranda, coupled with much arm waving and moving about, and forming and re-forming of little groups. But Regan was also studying other elements in the cameo view. The second floor had an exterior veranda, something he had not seen from street level. It was a sort of walkway that ran the four sides of the house. There was a man there, another large-built guy, walking that veranda, pacing it out, appearing and disappearing around the house, his paces as regular as a metronome's tick. So an armed guard at the gate. Presumably the veranda man was also armed. And six men in the rest of the house. How to grab this lot? How to raid this house, with its high walls and exit to the sea, and get both killer and his pals? And how to do it fast? And the biggest question of all, how to use this discovery to his advantage? Hijaz, Almadi, and the lot back in England, the Special Branch—they had all used him as a floor mop to wipe up various messes. The time had come for Regan to pay them all back, reshuffle the cards, and play a few deft hands of his own.

* * *

The English accent and the Mercedes worked. He managed to get a room at La Reserve in Beaulieu without luggage. He produced a story that his bags had been lost by British Airways at Nice Airport and received knowing nods. All he wanted was a room with a phone. La Reserve in Beaulieu attempts to rival all comers as the most expensive place to breathe air conditioning in the world. It would take some explaining when Regan stuck the Diners Club bill under the nose of Superintendent Maynon a month from now. Napoleon, or someone like that, had summed it up in an apt phrase—"There is no price to put on results." So Regan included in that a bottle of scotch to be sent to the room, a bottle of Evian, and a jug of ice. When that lot arrived he first poured a small sample mix, sat down, and picked up the phone.

"I'd like Hôtel du Cap, Eden Roc. 34.29.01."

"Please hold on, sir," the telephonist said. "We have a direct dial facility."

That was another reason Regan had selected an expensive hotel. He suspected that in order to cope with the nefarious French phone system he would need the help of an English-speaking French operator, and one was more likely to be obtainable at a pricey place.

"Hôtel du Cap."

"Monsieur Hijaz."

"Attendez, s'il vous plait."

A moment later Hijaz's voice came on the line. "Yes?"

"Me, Regan."

"Where did you go? You took a Mercedes away. What happened . . . ?" The man's voice was flat and worried as if he were sure the English cop had gotten up to mischief and he would get blamed for it.

"I spotted the man on the way back from that installation," Regan said gently. "The man who killed Haffasa in London. I followed him, found out where he and his pals live."

A pregnant silence for a moment, then Hijaz's voice came across so low it sounded like someone else's. "You've found the killer of bin Haffasa? You are sure?"

"He was following Almadi. I guess it was close."

"Where are you speaking from?" The question sharp, as if Hijaz was suddenly in a hell of a hurry.

Regan lifted the scotch and took a sip of it. He looked out through the open window of the elegant room. He couldn't see the villa from where he sat, but it was less than five hundred yards away. He sipped his drink, knowing it was not possible to hear the sound of somebody sweat, but in this case it was easy to imagine it.

"Where are you speaking from? Where is the Haffasa killer?" Hijaz's voice now higher and desperate.

Regan was silent for a full fifteen seconds and took another slug of scotch. Then he said, "Right, chummy, get yourself a piece of paper and pencil. But first get this. You learn nothing until you've made me a happy man. Right?" he snapped the word. "I resign the role of Number One Asshole. That's how I've been treated by you and your pals. You give me answers, you'll get the address. Part two is you don't give the answers to me, you give them to my superior in London. Or maybe he already has some of them, in which case you tell him to pass them along to me. Following all this?"

A half-strangled grunt at the end of the phone which Regan took as an affirmative.

"I think I've worked it out. It's political. It's big. It's got nothing to do with a guy going around blackmailing people. That's bullshit. This I suspect is governments, high-ranking politicians, that kind of area. And I, for reasons I don't know, was kicked into the middle of it. You listening to this?"

"Yes, yes," Hijaz said, all attentive.

"But now I have the ace. Here come the questions. Phone the answers to Superintendent Maynon, Flying Squad, New Scotland Yard, 01-230-1212. He'll check your answers. I can't do that from here. Question number one. Who was the guy in the red Jaguar who tried to kill me . . . ?"

"I can tell you now."

"I said tell Maynon. He'll check your answers. I can't," Regan said sharply. "Question two. What was the British Special Branch involvement in this case? Tell Maynon to let me have the truth. That seems to me to be a very gray area. No subtleties, no more fucking fiction or elaborations. I want the real story from whatever source it comes from, you or him."

"These are things I do not know about. . . ." Hijaz's voice seemed more frightened now than worried, a definite shift. Regan wondered about that.

"You're going to find out about that. Question three. What were those installations this morning? What's the deal Almadi's doing with the French government? Why is

the deal so important that first Haffasa was murdered to
try and stop it—and Almadi had a similar fate in store?"

"I can answer these questions if you come to Hôtel du
Cap."

"Question four. Who in hell are you, Hijaz? You're no
Bahrainian cop. I know cops worldwide. I'm saying you're
not a fucking cop, so what are you?"

The voice very low, almost a whisper. "Come to the
Hôtel du Cap."

"Speak to Maynon. Sort it out among yourselves. Tell
him I'll phone him in two hours from now. To get my
answers. Tell him if I suspect for one moment he's not
telling me the truth, I'll put the phone down, and you
won't get your killer. Clear?"

Regan didn't wait for the answer. He put the phone
down.

He killed the two-hour wait with three more scotches
and some out-of-date English newspapers in the hotel
lobby. He read the old stories, but his mind was somewhere else, not working out anything cogent, but imagin-
ing the wires humming all over London. Calls between
Scotland Yard, the foreign office, the House of Commons, maybe the cabinet, maybe the prime minister, the
lines hot with query and outrage, and maybe mystery. He
had a sense now of the outline without seeing the vital
detail; he could see the woods but not the trees. It was a
political caper; the intrigue and aggravation of it smelled

of intrigue at the highest level. A level so high that it had been thought to be beyond his ken, except that he was a top Yard cop whom they'd dropped into it. Their choice, not his. What was clear was that no one, from the second that he'd walked into his ACC's office at the Yard, had leveled with him. Well, now they must pay. If they wanted the guy who killed Haffasa, the going rate was the truth. The time had come to tell him the story, and the curious thing was that whatever the narrative, however complex or oblique or mad with subterfuge, he knew as soon as he heard the real story, he'd recognize it.

He put through the long-distance call to Scotland Yard at 6:00 P.M. Maynon came on the line in an ice-cold voice. "What is this, Regan? Are you threatening the British government? Is it blackmail? I warn you, this is tape recorded."

"Fine," Regan said gently. "I've worked out it's more than my job's worth. I've got the Haffasa killer, you've got some explaining. If you don't like that, accept my resignation. Do I put the phone down, or is it a deal . . . ?"

"I warn you that it's likely that disciplinary action will be taken against you on your return."

Regan's voice hardened. "There's no time left for that sort of talk, sir. Do I put the phone down, or do we talk?"

Regan got the truth. Superintendent Maynon kept it simple, although it was a complicated story. The ramifications surprised him. It contained elements he would not have guessed at, others which were so elemental he was angry he hadn't thought of them before. The explanations lasted about five minutes, including Regan's terse ques tions of clarification. But at the end of it he was satisfied. It was too oblique a story for anyone to have made up. The installation that Almadi's party and Regan had visited near Tende had been a new French atomic power station. New in every sense of the word, the installation had hardly started producing electricity and was the latest design in advanced gas-cooled reactor types. The secret deal that Almadi had come to France to make had been called by leading European politicians "the Deal of the Century." In return for the purchase of one billion dollars of French manufactured goods, ranging from textiles to Mirage jets, the French government was prepared to sell the Bahrainis four advanced gas-cooled reactor atomic power stations. Every leading politician in the world knew the significance of this deal. The Arabs didn't want the nuclear power stations to generate electricity. The cheapest way to make electricity is by burning oil—and the Arabs have all the oil they could ever want. The reason they were in France shopping for atomic power stations was that, as a result of the building of four atomic power stations in Bahrain by the French, the Arabs would be provided with the basic technology and materials to construct their first atomic bomb.

Meanwhile the Israelis had secretly had the atomic bomb now for the past three years. The great powers had been unable to stop Israel from building their bomb. But the same great powers, including Russia, had agreed that they didn't want the Arabs with a bomb. Arab politics were too volatile. The Israelis could be trusted not to start throwing the thing around, the Arabs not. That's what the

U.S., Russia, England, and India, four of the five world nuclear powers, had decided. The fifth, the French, had been in agreement with the others up to that moment in history when the Arabs turned the screws on Western civilization and introduced the blackmail politics of oil pricing.

There had been two results from this blackmail. The Arabs made a lot of money and enemies. The French leaders of a nation of shopkeepers, never slow to see an opportunity for profit, spotted the paradox, rich Arabs, poor in friendship. They started to study the spectrum of Arab needs. Number one on the East's shopping list was an atom bomb. The other nuclear powers said no, the Arabs were not to be trusted. The French decided that the Arab hierarchy, from Sadat to the young Harvard graduates who ran OPEC, currently seemed to have less screws loose than the politicos of Tel Aviv; and the real-politik of the situation was that atom bombs for all in the Middle East could be argued as giving a better balance of power.

The Arabs, according to Maynon, had approached all nuclear powers at one time or other looking for an atom power station purchase: the U.S., the Russians, Great Britain, India, and France. They'd all turned them down flat. Then in September 1975, the French had contacted a Bahraini representative and informed him that in exchange for a billion-dollar Arab deal with French industry, they would supply the very latest in nuclear power generating stations. The one condition of the sale was that the deal, up until delivery of the installation, should be kept secret.

The Arabs are not too good at secrets. By December 1975, Israeli intelligence knew all about it, and which Arabs were to meet which Frenchmen where, to make the deal.

The signature of contracts was to take place outside France. The first suggestion was the initial accord should be signed in London. Sheikh Hamid bin Haffasa was to check into the Wellington Clinic to hold a series of meetings with the French and sign the initial papers. The British government was aware of all this, was aware of the French deal with the Arabs, regretted it, but realistically there was nothing they could do about it. They could stop the papers being signed in London, but that would delay nothing. The papers could be signed at the Malta Hilton or the Excelsior, Rome.

Israeli intelligence, on the other hand, had different ideas. It informed the Iranian ambassador in Washington that any Arab who tried to sign any nuclear power station deal with the French would be assassinated. This gave certain Arabs food for thought. Haffasa decided to ignore the thought. He arrived in the Wellington Clinic, London, on March 7. On March 8 the man, who now sported a mustache and whom Maynon was identifying as a member of Israeli Intelligence, made his short but impressive visit to Haffasa's suite.

Had the British Special Branch been looking after Haffasa's security? That was one of Regan's questions.

"I've talked to the head of SB," Maynon answered. "They were notionally looking after Haffasa. The fact is the British government was not that keen on Haffasa's presence or business in England. The SB, I gather, had two guys on his security. They were obviously out for a quick one in St. John's Wood, center of the British pub industry, when chummy arrived with the M-38."

Regan said nothing but could see everything falling into place. Why the ACC had stuck him on the case. The logical outcome of the murder at the clinic should have been an inquiry into the SB—were they there or were they not? And if not, why? The Deal of the Century was going on and they knew about it—there should have been an armed man in every toilet. Except that the head of the SB had gotten feedback from English politicos that they were cool on the whole frog-wog deal. "Who was the guy in the red Jag?"

"Some Arab intelligence outfit," Maynon answered. "A low rating for those types—poor marks. I can only assume that the Jag driver thought you were present at the Wellington that morning as a killer returning to the scene of the crime, or some such. . . ."

"Some such . . ." Regan mused. "Yeah. When you think of the lack of finesse, lack of expertise of the attack, it smells like an Arab IU."

The chief superintendent had given him the answers. "Mr. Maynon, the Haffasa killer is in a villa. It's called Cap au Vent, Avenue Lille, St. Jean Cap Ferrat. I'm in a hotel about five hundred yards away, La Reserve. There are eight other men in the villa. My guess is they're all armed. I think we can take it. They're all part of an Israeli intelligence unit."

"Phone that man called Hijaz. Tell him the address. That was the deal," Maynon instructed.

Regan signed off with a couple of noncommittal pleasantries. But he didn't quite carry out Maynon's orders to the letter. He got the hotel switchboard to call the police prefecture at Antibes, who referred him to the Nice HQ. He talked to Inspector Guignard and told him about the men and the villa. Then he phoned Hôtel du Cap and talked to Hijaz, gave him the address, and also informed him that he'd given details to Guignard. Implicit in Regan's decision to talk to Guignard was that he felt he still could not trust Hijaz not to do something illegal or dangerous or stupid.

Hijaz didn't seem pleased at the variation in the deal. Maybe he'd had the idea of dropping the first Arabic atom bomb on a villa in Cap Ferrat before the French realized what was happening.

The raid was timed for 8:00 P.M. exactly. There was still light, though low clouds were piling up around the pinnacles of the mountain backdrop and beginning to slide down on the coast. Guignard probably calculated he had half an hour to get in, and to get out of the villa with its incumbents. Then it would be dark. If the Israelis put up resistance till night fell, Guignard must know there was a chance he'd lose some of them under cover of darkness.

It would be a technical arrest, though basically all Guignard wanted was to interrogate them, put the fresh-grown-mustache man on a twenty-four-hour hold while Regan and Scotland Yard assembled an extradition order.

The French police probe would go no further than that. There was no intention of pressing a criminal fugitive charge on the other seven for giving asylum to the killer. Basically the French detective and his superiors, maybe aided by a nod tipped from the Justice Ministry in Paris, just wanted the guys out of France; the killer on an arrest warrant Londonward, the others on El Al out of Nice Airport.

Guignard gave Regan explicit orders. Having taken a sworn statement from him at Nice HQ as to the killer's identification, he then ordered Regan to stay completely clear of the area of the raid.

Regan argued but got nowhere. At first he was angry, a natural enough reaction, especially as the phone in Guignard's office at the Nice headquarters kept on ringing and the French cop paid more attention to the phone than him. Then Regan relented. Guignard was taking fifteen armed men on the raid, and the point he was trying to make was that he couldn't guarantee Regan's safety if shooting started, nor the legal position if Regan shot someone or was shot at. Regan asked if he could be in the road outside the villa. The answer was no. He then asked if he could be on the police launch which would approach the villa from the sea side. Guignard gave another negative. He didn't want Regan any nearer to the scene than Hôtel La Reserve. Regan shrugged it off, and asked if Guignard could get him a pair of binoculars. He'd oversee the thing from the road between Beaulieu and Villefranche. Guignard's assistant produced an expensive pair of Leitz binoculars. At half-past seven Guignard person ally dropped Regan back at La Reserve. Regan got into the Mercedes and drove back to the spot with the view down five hundred yards to the villa on Cap Ferrat.

The light was going, but streetlights were twinkling on along the coast roads and avenues out on Cap Ferrat. Some neon from the Beaulieu Casino and other arcades was reflecting out across the water. Regan saw the boat at two minutes to eight coming fast around the corner from Nice and heading across Villefranche Bay and moving in directly to the villa's mooring steps. Regan was impressed by the speed and precision with which the French cops were out of the boat, up the steps, and fanned out around the grounds of the house within seconds. They made a lot of noise on landing. Regan could hear the shouts across the narrow stretch of water.

The villa had been quiet. Lights were on in two of the lower rooms and one of the upper bedrooms. As the cops arrived from the sea and hit the lawns, lights seemed to go on all over the house, and doors were opening and people shouting, most of this drowned out by the simultaneous arrival of three gendarme cars, Klaxons hee-hawing across the railway bridge onto the peninsula. Regan heard a crash. He couldn't see the front gates from his position, but it sounded like one of the cop cars hadn't waited for the guard to open the gates. Only seconds after the sea-borne gendarmes hit the back lawn, he could see other armed uniformed cops racing around from the front of the villa.

He head the crackle of automatic rifle fire. Several long bursts, then half a dozen isolated shorter bursts. It was impossible to work out what the firing was about, possibly Guignard's men loosing off warning shots. There was now more light spilling from the villa as cops penetrated inside and began a sweep of each floor. Then Regan saw some of them stepping out onto a balcony on the second floor. He'd just seen two other cops on the first-floor veranda. The gendarmerie were now throughout the house. He panned his binoculars down to the main room at the rear of the ground floor, in time to see an officer draw the curtains and slide open a long picture window. Regan saw the archetype cameo of French cops strutting about prodding the eight huge guys with their pistols, lining them up, cautioning them to keep their hands on their heads.

The whole operation had taken less than three minutes from the arrival on the mooring steps to Regan seeing the figure of Guignard leading his group with the eight men, sandwiched in the middle of it, onto the lawn. A couple of police vans then appeared from around the front of the villa. The Israeli group was loaded in.

He drove into Nice and back to the gendarmerie headquarters in Avenue de France. Guignard kept him hanging around for half an hour, then came back and organized an office from which he could phone Scotland Yard. When he got through, Regan spoke to the duty officer, Squad Office, and asked him to start the motions with the home office for extradition papers. Guignard found a bottle of scotch and gave Regan a generous helping. The French CID man also assigned one of his sergeants to go back to La Reserve in Beaulieu, collect Regan's bill, and deliver it to the Hôtel du Cap.

It was 9:45 P.M. There was nothing much for Regan to do now except to drink the scotch and say his good-byes. He asked, just so that he could note on any subsequent report, for facilities at some time in the near future to interview the Wellington Clinic killer. The man's name was now known—at least he carried a passport issued to a "Ben Allon." Regan requested to interview Allon briefly and was surprised to find that the eight men had in fact not been brought to the Nice prefecture, but were apparently overnighting it in the cells of Beaulieu's gendarmerie.

"We had a big drug bust earlier today, fifteen arrests in Nice, four in Cannes," Guignard told Regan. "Our cells are full."

"I should see Ben Allon. I should identify him face to face before extradition."

"Okay tomorrow? There's no hurry. You won't get your extradition papers for some time."

Regan left the Nice prefecture with unresolved worry about the evening's proceedings. He was concerned about the legal technicality of starting the process of extradition of a man whom he hadn't actually spoken to yet.

He could have stayed the night in La Reserve; he'd already paid for the room. But he went back to Hôtel du Cap, because it was nearer to Nice, and he felt like running up a few more expenses on Almadi's bill. Also he wanted to check on Hijaz. Hijaz had been conspicuous by his absence at the villa raid tonight. Guignard had told Regan that he'd warned Hijaz, as well as Regan, off. Regan was surprised that Hijaz had obeyed the order.

He drove the Mercedes back to Hôtel du Cap and dumped it in the forecourt. It was 10:00 P.M. when he walked into the foyer of the hotel. The clerk gave him his key and a single sheet of paper. On it was scrawled, "Miss you. Where are you? Jo," and the day's date. He'd totally forgotten her, written her off. He'd decided she was unobtainable and yet here she was, leaving a note for him. He'd dismissed her last night as he sat in the car outside the restaurant the Oasis. Evidently his cursory addition of the fors and againsts had come out wrong. Why had he made such a decision? He picked up the house phone and dialed her extension. At least he hadn't forgotten that. She answered the phone immediately, like she had been waiting there to pounce on it. "It's me, Jack."

"Terrific," she said very softly.

"Can you get away?"

"Your room. Five minutes, okay?"

"Yes." He replaced the phone.

She was there in four minutes.

He opened the door, she walked in, turned, and moved into his arms. They kissed. She held him, tightly at first, then relaxed.

"I should have phoned. I'm sorry," he said.

"Don't talk before we're in bed." Then suddenly she looked anxious. Maybe she thought she'd come on, opened, too strong.

She was wearing a simple green silk dress. It looked like something she couldn't have afforded, so perhaps it was a gift from her Arab mentor. It had six silk-covered buttons running down between her breasts. Regan undid them, then helped her step out of the dress.

They made love quickly, like a warm-up. Then Regan drank some scotch. They made love again, this time with the windows open and the half-moon witness to acts of virility and powers of charm. Somewhere else in the hotel a dog started barking. Regan and Jo almost unaware of anything extraneous to their four walls, their own bodies, and Regan's gentle deaths on top of her. The whole performance virtually wordless from the moment she walked into his arms.

She turned on the light to study his naked body as he got up. He poured another scotch and lit a smoke. He nodded toward the toilet facilities. She shook her head.

He sat down by her on the bed. She borrowed a pull on his cigarette, then a sip of his drink.

"I watched you in that restaurant the other night. . . ."

"Oasis?"

"You looked so beautiful. I gave you up. A lost cause."

"I don't understand." Her fingernails began to stroke in around his thighs.

"Almadi, the world's richest lover. That's your speed. The world's top millionaires just to sweep the court for your play. So what the hell are you doing in bed with me?" He asked it like it was a purely practical question.

"Well. you work it out. . . ." She was smiling, a genuine happy look. "I like you. You want something, you go and get it. You wanted me, you took me. These people are just spenders. Nothing else. From my point of view that has more limitations than attractions. There's a high turnover of girls in this Almadi type of world. They come with nothing, have a helluva time, go with nothing. At least I have a house in Pinner."

"Pinner? What d'you mean, house in Pinner?" Regan was puzzled by the sudden change of tack. Pinner didn't seem to have anything to do with the conversation.

"I got something out of it for my old age. I took their money and I bought a house in Pinner, northwest London, suburban housewife belt. . . ."

"I know Pinner."

"You bloody well would." She laughed. "You bloody well would know Pinner. How many raids have you carried out on the mid-morning widows of Pinner with a condom grabbed from the husband's store . . . ?"

Regan gently pushed her back onto the bed. "That's criminal libel," he said, teeth clenched. "I want to come and live with you in Pinner, or wherever."

"Lovely," she said. "Now just shut up and be physical."

He knew the signs. It would become serious. So he should decide now, 11:00 P.M. at night. Pull out tomorrow, never see her again, or take the plunge, commit the lot. He hadn't met a girl quite like this before. That gave him an unusual problem, confusion.

They were getting up and getting dressed because he had decided to go into Beaulieu to the police prefecture and see Ben Allon. She had decided—he was against it—but she had decided she was going with him. They were quiet, stumbling into clothes, drunk on physical exhaustion. He was aware of her body as she put on, or pulled up, the bits and pieces to re-cover her nakedness. She was beautifully made, faultless. There was no other verdict.

They were quiet too in the Merc on the way into Beaulieu. She put her head against his shoulder and may have dozed. He concentrated on the mix of his driving and thoughts of her.

Well, it hadn't been the first time in his life that he'd collided with a beautiful girl. There'd been his wife. People were always surprised about that, especially his superiors at the Yard, that he'd gotten it away with a girl as classy as that one. A body that stuck out in exactly the right places within millimeters of perfection. English rose face, pert and fresh and full of youth. That was before the baby. One baby and the face had put on eight years. Nonetheless Kate was still good looking.

There had been Christa on that case in New York a year back, a bird of sexual ambivalence whom he could have straightened out if his personal history had been stabilized at the time. But no, he was in the normal quandary of his life with the added problem that the New York case had specialized in the kinds of straws that break camels' backs. Christa had been lovely—but always unobtainable. A gringo career bird as undetachable from New York as an ancient mess of flyswat on a wall. Jo was different. First of all he could understand her. Sure, she was living the fantasy of heavy money and the sheikhs of

Araby. But it was a practical fantasy. She was charging a fee. London was populated by girls who did it for nothing, for a meal, sometimes just breakfast or a roof over their heads for the night. There were two ways of describing the girl whose head rested on his shoulder. She was a whore, or she was someone who'd gotten it together, collected the checks, saved for the future, and meanwhile managed a variation of the life of Riley. Regan's mind was on that bent.

The car moved down the back of Nice, heading for the coast road again, and he realized he was on the wrong track. The only thing that concerned him really was whether it was a going proposition. He now wanted it to be. The simple question was whether a girl like this would want to settle in with him. There would be problems. Problems now, and future problems. But nothing was ever insuperable while it worked, while there was care and need. The main thing was that she'd seriously said yes, that she wanted to see him back in London. She was maybe twenty-two, twenty-four—he'd never asked her age, yet she wanted him, a guy decompressing fast into the forty-year-old diver's bends and blackout, where the enemy is not that there's no youth in the morning, but less wish for it, less capability to cope with it, outright failure of a forty-year-old cop to amaze and entertain a girl almost half his age, the age of a daughter. Regan knew it was not possible to fob a young girl off—"I'm working late tonight, big thieving job in Peckham, enjoy your knitting." He'd kicked a marriage in the face with that type line. So what prospects, he asked himself, as he nosed the

Merc through the late night, motorized drunks circling the port, heading themselves out for Villefranche, Beaulieu, and Monaco. What prospects for the cop and the beautiful whore in Pinner? It was the limbs, legs, hands, the heart. Senses rather than sums, intuitions not equations. All those said yes—any madness is possible. He confessed to himself now, on an ill-lit road somewhere in darkest France, that for years he'd been looking for a girl to really live with. Well, he'd found her—this head on his shoulder. And he was suddenly sure he would find the ways to make it work.

Later he was to try and remember the sequence of what exactly happened second by second from the time they arrived at the prefecture in Beaulieu to the moment the shooting started. There were reasons for this. First, he'd have to make detailed reports for the Yard, line up the facts along a time sequence. Second, the French police at a later date required his facts for their investigation. Third, he needed the sequence of times and decisions for his own purposes. He needed to know, because he was going to have to live with the nightmare for the rest of his life, what he could have done to have prevented it, curtailed or confined it, when the killings started. What exactly did he himself do second by second, and which, if any, of his moves was critically culpable? It had started so fast, doors had burst open, windows had exploded, lacing their glass onto linoleum floors. There were probably, in combination, a hundred things he could have done had he selected certain decisions. And yet they died, all of them. He needed the sequence to answer the question—had he fucked up? A vitally important, private question. Ever since he'd joined the Flying Squad he'd been aware that a metronome paced the seconds, and somehow they were all borrowed. And one day the ticking would stop. Then the brief pause before the time bomb went off. In the midst of a thousand violent situations in his seventeen years as a cop, he had made his decisions. But he'd always known one day one decision would turn out his personal disaster. When that happened, and if he survived it, he knew he'd make the decision to leave the police. The events in Beaulieu prefecture that night put him close to that decision.

Other reasons why he had to make a sequential split-second breakdown of events. It was to be a big story, the Beaulieu raid. It would make some part of the front page of most world newspapers. The French Justice Ministry wanted his role made clear. The crime related to a Scotland Yard investigation into a killing in London—the Midi police were unprepared because they were uninformed; their confreres in London had failed to fill them in. So he would go back over the events at Beaulieu many times and for different reasons. How it started was not difficult to recall. What exactly happened to everybody inside the prefecture from the moment the balloon went up was more difficult if not impossible to get exactly straight.

He and Jo had arrived at the prefecture at about 11:30 P.M. The prefecture was next to the railway station in the lower of the town's two squares. Regan parked alongside the tourist information hut. He chatted to Jo for a minute about protocol. He told her he thought the best thing was for her to wait in the Mercedes. He'd go inside and check that Ben Allon and the seven other Israelis were still in the cells. Then he would mention to the incumbent inspector that a woman who was germane to the case was sitting in a car outside and he'd like permission to bring her in. He said he didn't anticipate any problems. He just felt it was bad form for a Yard inspector to walk unannounced into a French nick with a beautiful girl on his arm. Very French, but not good form.

Jo agreed, and Regan got out of the car. He walked the fifty paces to the front door of the double-storied building. The doors were closed. He went up four steps and rang a bell. There was an inquiry in French. He gave his name. The doors opened. He walked inside.

A young sergeant led him to the duty room, four doors down the hall on the left. Other doors were open. He reckoned there were about six cops in the place. Another sergeant in the duty room made an internal phone call and he was then taken upstairs to an office immediately at the top of the stairs and introduced to a Chief Inspector Lassigny. The French detective spoke good English. Regan told him he wanted to make a quick pass at the prisoner Allon, inform him of the extradition charges pending, and ask him a few questions which would probably gain nothing in the way of answers but would give him, Regan, a chance to size up the bloke, see if he could spot the pressure points. He hoped that Lassigny could help him with facilities for a lengthy interrogation session tomorrow.

Lassigny looked more like a French paratrooper than a cop. His face was hard, the eyes coldly alert and glinting as if they contained slivers of steel to catch the light. He walked in measured steps with a stiff back. He took Regan downstairs to the cells, guarded by an old sergeant with food stains on the collar of his blue serge uniform. Somehow Regan didn't want to start the Jo number on Lassigny. The French cop would likely gather that Jo was no more than Regan's girlfriend and would not be impressed at the Yard man's mixing pleasure casually in with this most important case.

There were eight cells in the Beaulieu prefecture, which suited the Nice HQ requirements after the villa raid. One man to each cell. The retired sergeant with the food stains on his clothes sat at a trestle table by the door. A submachine gun leaned against the wall by him. With a bunch of keys that looked like something out of a medieval castle, Lassigny opened the door to Allon's cell. He gestured Regan to go before him into the cell.

Regan entered. The man was lying on a brick-and-tiled bench with a wooden-slat top. He sat up, looked them over, and said nothing.

Regan checked his memory of his last view of this man—the elevator in the Wellington Clinic. It was Haffasa's executioner. "You speak English?" he asked.

The man shrugged.

"You know what you're being charged with?"

"I have committed no crime in France."

His English was good, the voice softly made, as if his career had been spent persuading rather than ordering people.

"You're to be extradited to London, where you'll stand trial for the murder of a man called Haffasa."

Allon gave Regan a practical look. "When?"

"A few days. Meanwhile you'll be answering a few questions I'll be putting to you. . . ."

The man smiled.

"I'll want to know about your group. Whether you acted independently, or whether the clinic killing was a conspiracy."

"I'm not much of a talker," Allon said gently.

"I've never interrogated a man who thought he was going to tell me something. You'll talk to me. We'll do some kind of deal, and you'll talk. Tomorrow we'll talk."

The man shrugged.

"See you in the morning," Regan said quietly.

He and Lassigny left the cells and climbed the stairs to the mezzanine. "I'd like an office for tomorrow."

"Follow me," Lassigny said.

They moved down the corridor to the last room on the right.

The went inside. It was a bare room, windowless, one battered folding table, one chair, and a single overhead bulb.

"So what d'you think of Allon?" Lassigny asked.

Regan hadn't made up his mind. "Not a thug. Educated. He'll be a problem. But we'll solve it."

"I don't think he'll talk."

"He'll talk," Regan said matter-of-factly. "When d'you put his friends on a plane to Tel Aviv?"

"In the morning. 0800 hours."

Suddenly there was the noise of all hell breaking loose in the hall outside. The submachine guns started firing together, barking out their own noise and the screamed whines of ricocheting shells and splintering wood. It must have been that Lassigny couldn't believe that his prefecture was under attack.

The man must have thought that for some bizarre reason it was cops out in the hall, shooting into the street. Lassigny stepped out into the hall. Regan saw the front of his uniform shred in an explosion of cloth and blood as the man jerked backward with the impact of the submachinegun fire. Regan's automatic reaction was to step out and grab the man as he fell. The burst of bullets ended in a metallic scraping and a click which he identified as someone just outside the front door pulling the spent magazine out of the M-38 that had killed Lassigny, replacing it with a fresh magazine. Regan laid the dead man on the floor and took a quick look out and saw the killer standing on the steps outside, lit by the hall lights.

He was a tall man with a florid red face and thick black eyebrows. He was fumbling and snapping the new magazine into his gun. As he stood there, two others of his gang came up behind him. Regan stepped back into the office as the others opened fire. A bullet or ricochet blew the main neon fitting apart, and suddenly everything was in darkness. The raiders paused. Regan saw his first and possibly last opportunity to make a move. He catapulted himself out of the room and up the stairs. He had a reason for this instant choice of action and direction. Lassigny was the senior cop in the prefecture—his office would probably double for the station armory. Regan had seen a large cupboard immediately behind the man's desk. He'd only spotted one gun inside the building so far. It belonged to the sergeant on cell duty. It was important to get a weapon for himself, and with some luck get weapons into the hands of the other gendarmes.

He reached the top of the stairs and threw himself through the door into Lassigny's office. He rushed to the cupboard and grabbed its doors opened. It was an ordnance cupboard, but inside the racks were bare. Regan cursed, turned, and pulled out the four drawers of Lassigny's desk—no revolvers. He ran out of the office along the corridor to a window at its bottom that looked out over the station square. He was just in time to see three men, stockings over their faces, all armed, run into the downstairs hall, firing continuously. But in the half-light of the square he saw other figures, the glint of gunmetal, maybe four more gunmen out there and that not including the shadowy shapes of three more behind the wheels of Citroen ID 19's. The lights on the cars were out, but their engines were revving high.

He heard shots and screams mixed up with French oaths. Below him, in rooms off the hall, gendarmes were dying. Footsteps running all over the shop except up the stairs. And what move could he make? He ran back to the stairwell at the top of the stairs. Someone heard his footfalls—some raider down in the hall—but didn't come after him. His target would not be upstairs, but he started firing crazily upward to warn off anyone up there. The ceiling above his head exploded and snowed down in a cloud of dust. He had made the wrong move. When Lassigny had died, Regan should have gone downstairs to the cells, not upstairs. He should have gone for the old sergeant's submachine gun. Now he heard more shots and screams. There was thirty seconds' worth of firing and then a single isolated moment of dead silence. Then a series of bursts, eight of them. And Regan knew why there were exactly eight bursts.

He stood poised just around from the top of the stairs. The men of the raiding party were running up from the cells, milling in the hallway, firing at random into the ground-floor rooms, then running out into the square, still firing. And still he was paralyzed, impotent, because he was unarmed, unable to find a gun. There was no way at all to stop this execution party with commands, words, reason. Had he tried that, it would have been his suicide.

He didn't understand why there was a further burst of firing from the square. There was no sound now from inside the station. He could hear the murderers' footfalls across the cobbles, the running of the Citroen engines, the anguished scream of powered tires as they took off. But in between all that a burst of machine-gun fire not aimed at the prefecture. Then suddenly he was running headlong down the stairs and across the hallway. In his haste he missed one of the four steps down onto the cobbles and tripped, slid, felt searing pain as his knees cracked on the cobbles, but got up, all one movement. But already he knew it was too late.

She'd seen their attack on the prefecture. She must have seen or simply heard the killing. She must have been rooted in the passenger seat of the Merc with fear and indecision for the brief minutes of the massacre. And then she had made her move. She had known that Regan was inside the building. She had headed for the building with God knows what ideas in her mind—to try to protect him? Or maybe she recognized someone in the raiding party. Or maybe she thought she could do something, anything. She was in love, and he was inside, and men were killing in there. She had gotten out of the Mercedes and started toward the prefecture. She must have collided with them as they came out, their work done. Maybe she had tried to grapple one of them. Maybe they shot her simply because she was present, a witness. But they killed her. Jo lay on the cobbles and Regan got down and cradled her head, but one look at her face and he could see that it was too late; already the life had seeped out of her body.

He was stunned. He looked around the empty square. No movement there, the sound of the getaway cars still echoing in the distance. His eyes minutely probed the darkness looking for someone, some human contact, to unload his scream of hatred and incomprehension upon. It was not conceivable that this had happened, but it had. She and Lassigny and others murdered within seconds, the pall of death still drifting in the light dust of broken wall and ceiling plaster around the splintered front doors of the prefecture.

He laid her head back on the cobbles and then he was running. Because it was only seconds from her death, and the three getaway cars could still be heard, and he'd seen something hanging by a strap on a nail behind the desk in the duty room. He ran into the prefecture and into the duty room.

He hardly gave the three dead gendarmes in the room a glance. He grabbed the binoculars and ran out again.

He ran past her body out into the middle of the square. He put the binoculars to his eyes and started to pan them around, a full 360-degree pan, exploring the darkness of the terraces and buildings of the slopes of Beaulieu, poorly lit by the streetlamps and house lights.

This job would have been ordered up. These assassins would have flown in singly or in pairs from various cities, Beirut, Tangier, Bahrain, Athens, in the last four hours. What Regan was searching the streets for was the man who'd put in the order to attack the prefecture and kill the Israeli commandos. He put the binoculars to his eyes. That man, having made this arrangement, would have come to Beaulieu and taken up a secret position within sight of the prefecture to watch whether his plan had worked out. Regan would bet his life on it.

He panned the the binoculars around the town and into the upper square. People were already gathering on the streets, moving down now to investigate the noise of gunfire and speeding cars. Lights, in a chiaroscuro of patterns, burned on in every occupied flat and villa. But he wasn't looking for people heading into the square, he was looking for someone heading away. He had just pointed the binoculars at the west edge of the town when he saw something. He tight-focused the capstan on the top of the instrument. He saw a Mercedes heading back for Nice. He couldn't at first identify its one occupant, the driver. But then the man's profile and the polish of his bald head were suddenly caught in the lights of an oncoming car. It was Hijaz. The Mercedes disappeared from view behind the ribbon of roadside villas.

They were the longest most frustrating moments of his life, trying to phone the Hôtel du Cap, trying to get through to Guignard at Nice prefecture. Guignard was too busy to talk to him, Guignard was anchored to his phone questioning the one gendarme survivor of the Beaulieu raid. Finally Regan got to a phone in the nearby Metropole Hotel and rang Hôtel du Cap. He left a message with Sheikh Almadi's private secretary. The man had problems understanding the message, but Regan insisted that he repeat it until he'd got it right. The message was for Hijaz, and it simply stated that he, Regan, would shortly be coming to Hôtel du Cap to arrest him for the Beaulieu murders.

He went back to the Beaulieu prefecture and did manage to talk on the phone to Guignard. Guignard told him there were five carloads of gendarmes on the way, and roadblocks set up.

"Forget the roadblocks, you won't get this lot. I've never seen anything so professionally organized. These men will have disappeared into thin air," Regan said.

Guignard snorted his disagreement and asked Regan what he wanted.

Regan explained that he'd seen Hijaz at Beaulieu. "I want some of your men at Nice Airport. If Hijaz attempts to leave the country for any destination other than London, where he left his private jet, have him arrested.

Otherwise, let him go to London, but inform me of the flight details."

"I'll send men immediately." Guignard replaced the phone before Regan took up any more of his time.

Several ambulances had arrived outside the prefecture. They took Jo's body first. Regan went outside, but they had already put her body into the ambulance and closed its doors. The van moved off. Regan walked back into the prefecture and tried to think of any sort of activity so that he would forget about her. He needed to make cold calculations now—he must not let his growing murderous rage overtake him.

An hour later Guignard phoned. Hijaz had left Nice Airport on a chartered twin-engined Cessna for London. A clerk at the British Airways desk had helped him to phone Heathrow Airport with instructions to refuel the Boeing 727 and have it ready taxiing for takeoff on his arrival.

Regan then phoned the Yard, told them he would be back in London first thing in the morning, and left precise instructions for the reception party to meet Hijaz.

Of course they blew it—the Yard officers' meeting with Hijaz at the airport. He must have made another phone call from Nice. There were two senior men from the Bahrain embassy and a leading London lawyer at Heathrow when the Cessna touched down. What exactly happened next was confusing. Detective Chief Inspector Pallin of the Flying Squad had arrived with four men. He was intercepted and briefly questioned by the lawyer before he could get to Hijaz, who had been advised to wait it out for the moment and say nothing in the VIP lounge of Terminal One. The lawyer then phoned a senior official at the home office, and Pallin had to explain the position over the phone—that on the instructions of a squad DI at present in France, this man was to be arrested on a nonspecific charge and held, pending the return of the officer from France in the morning. Pallin was then asked a number of questions. Had he received a Telex or phoned corroboration from a senior French police source specifically naming Hijaz in connection with the Beaulieu gendarmerie massacre? Did Pallin have an extradition order in the event that Hijaz turned around and went back to France? According to DI Regan, the man was implicated in a killing in the Wellington Clinic; what evidence was there to substantiate proceedings in the event of a writ of habeus corpus being produced by this man's distinguished lawyer? Finally, was Pallin aware of the extreme sensitivity of any dealings with the Arab world, one of the largest single creditors of the British government? Also there was the technicality of the arresting officer being abroad—Pallin was merely acting as a proxy. As there was no one currently in the Yard who had any evidence to back this DI Regan's accusations, and DI Regan was not making these accusations within the United Kingdom mainland, and was therefore not technically answerable under English law of false arrest, then he, the home office official, while not doubting for one moment the news of the Beaulieu massacre, would strongly advise Pallin that he should not willy-nilly arrest a senior Arab state official until this DI Regan reappeared with the goods. The home office official recommended that Pallin escort Mr. Hijaz to wherever he was going in London, a hotel or the embassy, and then keep tabs on him till Regan arrived.

Chief Inspector Pallin was concerned because his orders had come down from Superintendent Maynon. It was 1:30 in the morning. He called the Yard and got them to phone Maynon's home number, but there was no reply.

Meanwhile, as the lawyer was gently reasoning with the police about the state of affairs, Hijaz was becoming more excitable and angry. He had stepped off a private plane to find an English policeman trying to arrest him on a murder charge—his initial bluster had turned to shock, then anger. He refused to speak English. The two men from the embassy had more problems in trying to restrain him than Pallin. After half an hour of gradually mounting histrionics, the officials and Pallin managed to convince him that he was not going to be allowed to get on his Boeing and fly out of the country. He was not technically being arrested but he was not being allowed for the moment to leave. The police were prepared to accompany him to the embassy or a residence.

Hijaz finally calmed down. He didn't want to go to the embassy. He told the embassy officials he would go to an apartment in North Square, Bayswater. He got angry again when they relayed the address to Pallin.

Pallin and the four cops in two cars trailed the embassy Rolls-Royce from the now almost empty airport through the night into a deserted London.

It was 2:20 by the time the party reached North Square. The Rolls stopped outside Number Eleven, a large house newly converted into three maisonettes. There was a For Sale notice on the railings outside the house advertising second- and top-floor flats. Hijaz alone got out of the car, climbed the three steps, produced a key, and opened the front door. He disappeared inside, and lights came on behind closed curtains on the ground floor. The embassy Rolls went off into the night with the lawyer and the two officials.

Pallin phoned through on his radio/transceiver for another squad car. He had to have enough men to guard both the front and rear of the building. He asked that the men be armed, which was good thinking. Hijaz had decided to go to an address in North Square, Bayswater, because he knew there was a gun there.

The plane slowed, wallowed around for a moment in some cirrus turbulence, circled the cloud-blistered ceiling of West London, and headed down. Regan felt his pulse quicken, his stomach tighten against the safety belt. He had found over the last two hours on the flight from Nice the control he was looking for—a kind of ice-cool serenity isolating his emotional from his rational mind. He needed the rational for thinking, planning. He needed the emotional set apart, for the final decision, which would have everything to do with the death of Jo and the others massacred in Beaulieu. There had been a VHF message from the Yard to the radio operator of the

British Airways flight. It said simply, "Suspect Hijaz at 11 North Square Bayswater under armed surveillance." So the Met had blown out at London Airport. It didn't surprise him. The home office always adopted a general wet look as soon as anyone came up with the game of Grab the Diplomat. Anyhow they had him sewn up in London under armed surveillance. That was good enough.

He felt the air whistle out of the cabin as the plane depressurized. The Trident rocked a couple of times like a drunken racehorse, then touched down with protest and backbiting and the almighty roar of reversed engines. He was home in London, his domain, where he held sway. Here he gave orders, he knew the ropes, all of them, and how to pull them, and how to twine them into a hangman's cord. For the last few days in the south of France he'd felt like a spare man at a wedding. Well, now it would be different. London was his manor. He did what he liked in this town—even when his superiors stepped in and ordered him to do something one way, he'd never taken that to preclude doing the exact opposite. He knew a few tricks in this town of London, knew all of them, in fact. The current commissioner of the Metropolitan Police might think that Hijaz was secure and surrounded in a maisonette in Bayswater. As far as Regan was concerned, Hijaz was impaled on his spider's web and, very simply, was about to be consumed.

The plane halted, and he pushed his way off it. No time for manners now—not a second to be wasted on irrelevancies. He shoved his Met ID into the face of a Customs man, who signaled him as he went through the green exit from the Customs Hall. The man waved him on. Regan would have blasted him if he'd tried any of the usual pathetic Customs officer stunts.

A car was waiting. Not his usual car with Len Roberts driving, but Haskins's driver in a Volvo Estate—a new squad acquisition, engine mildly overheating. They drove into London at ninety. At the Yard Regan looked at his watch for the first time since getting off the plane: 10:22. It was almost as if looking at the time might spoil his concentration. Time didn't matter, the fly was in the web—now to prepare the meal.

He'd asked on the plane's VHF for an urgent meeting with the assistant commissioner of crime, and the ACC had agreed. Regan took the elevator up to the fifth floor, and then walked left along the corridor to the center of the building, where the ACC had his office suite. The assistant commissioner of crime was named Huggueson, pronounced "Hewson." Regan had always pronounced it "Hugson." He did not have to wait in the ACC's outer office; the secretary gestured for him to go straight in.

Regan walked in and gave a nod to the tall, distinguished man behind the desk. "Good morning, sir," he said, "this is what I want . . ."

What he wanted was the lot, complete charge of the Hijaz surveillance arrangements pending his deposition of evidence linking Hijaz to the Beaulieu killings. There was also a second charge relating to Hijaz's involvement in a murder attempt on Regan by the driver of a red Jaguar in the U.K. The ACC granted him the overall charge of surveillance, provided he would dictate a report right away—the commissioner must be fully briefed by the time the Bahrain embassy came back with its heavy guns. Meanwhile the ACC called in his secretary and gave her three names in the Paris police commission and the Justice Ministry for her to phone. Regan also said it would be useful for him to talk to Guignard, and Huggueson added the name to the secretary's list.

Regan walked down one floor to Squad Office and along to his office. Nothing had changed, a pile of mail and some new files on his desk, and a couple of dozen telephone messages. He avoided looking at them. He unlocked his equipment cupboard and got out a Philips Stenorette, closed the door, sat down, phoned the switchboard, told the duty operator no calls, replaced the phone, and concentrated. He fine-tuned his mind to short sentences, to get the whole thing explained, but briefly. He was now extremely anxious to get out to North Square. But he appreciated the ACC's point of view. They had to know the full story. He dictated it in the formal, spare, flat style of police reports. He began with the first visit to the Wellington Clinic, and finished with his return from France and his appointment as officer in charge at surveillance site. He had just started to itemize his thoughts on the possible range of legal procedures against Hijaz, the pros and cons of perhaps extraditing him to France, and, separately, the necessity for a prolonged interrogation if the names of the group who raided the prefecture were to be established, when the phone rang shrilly right at his elbow. He picked it up. "I said no fucking calls."

A hesitation, then Haskins's voice cold, but not affronted. "ACC says you're duty officer, North Square. I've just been informed that three unidentified men entered the maisonette ten minutes ago. Five minutes ago, Hijaz, armed with a gun, accompanied by the three, tried to leave the house by a rear garden door. Hijaz fired at a constable who attempted to intercept, then retreated back into the house. . . ."

"Christ." Regan was already standing.

"The PC has shoulder wounds, a bullet in the lung, not too seriously injured."

"I'm going there." Regan dropped the phone back on its cradle. It missed the cradle and fell to the floor. But he didn't see that because he was already out of the office.

It was a small square, less than sixty houses cluttered around a plot of grass abused by dogs and contained by black railings, mostly broken. The facades on two sides of the square were Edwardian, the third side fifties modern where a row of houses had been demolished after bomb damage. The south side of the square was Victorian— fewer and larger houses with short gardens and a mews lane at the back. The row was bisected by a narrow road leaving the square and filtering down through the backup of small, one-way streets to the main artery, the Bayswater Road at its east end near Marble Arch. Hijaz was in a corner house on the south side, where the narrow road met the square. So in fact the house could be overlooked, overseen, from three sides.

The first thing that Regan saw when he arrived was the gray face of the injured policeman. He hadn't been moved from the mews entrance, back of the house, probably within yards of where Hijaz's bullets had cut him down. The docs had gotten the man's shirt off, installed a drip, and were now slowly propping him up with blankets and pillows on the stretcher, to make him comfortable for the lift into the ambulance and the journey to the hospital. They were also looking for the exit holes of the bullets. Four had gone in, two had come out. Haskins had been wrong. Regan knew a seriously injured man when he saw one. This constable was in a touch-and-go situation.

He spent a minute with the small crowd around the stretcher, including press photographers, then was off to prowl the square. Five times he stopped to introduce himself to various confreres. He said his line—he was DI Regan, officer in charge. There had been about twenty uniformed cops in the square when he'd arrived. By the time he almost completed his tour, he'd spotted another six prowl cars arrive. More would be turning up now like bees to a honey pot. The news would be across the police radio bands that a cop had been shot in Bayswater.

Most of the men Regan introduced himself to knew him either by name or by reputation. Then a Special Patrol group arrived—the best the SPG could round up suddenly at 10:45 A.M. was twenty cops in one of its buses, all armed. Regan knew Harris, the guy heading the group. Regan gave him his opinion: hang back from the square, concentrate on security in depth, and crowd con trol. Show their arms to the public. There was now a problem with the public. This immediate Bayswater area was bedsitter and small-hotel country. Fortunately the row of Victorian houses where Hijaz and company were holed up seemed to be still private houses. The police had already evacuated the south side of the square within ten minutes of the shooting incident.

A mobile control unit Leyland van arrived from the Yard. Regan got into the back of the van, took up a microphone, and started to issue a series of terse orders.

The first thing he organized was the cutting off of the electricity supply to the siege house. A police van was positioned between the house and the electricity manhole cover in the road. Three policemen, armed with Remington rifles, moved in with two London Electricity Board men. They stood by the men in the sheltering cover of the van while they removed the manhole cover and switched off the electricity for the whole south side of the square. While this was being done, a constable found a flat on the top floor of a house on the north side of the square which had easy access to the roof. Regan sprinted across to the north side, climbed four flights of stairs, and got out onto the roof.

He had obtained a pair of binoculars from Inspector Harris. Now he looked across the square to the Hijaz house. The curtains were drawn in all of the windows of Hijaz's flat. There were no curtains in the windows of the second- and top-floor apartments for sale. But just as Regan was about to put down the binoculars he saw a movement in a room in the second-floor apartment. The man Regan had glimpsed for a split second in the hall of the Beaulieu prefecture, the man with florid face and thick eyebrows who had shot Lassigny and then stood on the front steps changing the magazine on his M-38, stepped into the room. He saw there were no curtains in the room and immediately retreated. The whole action took less than two seconds. But it was enough for Regan to know that some of the men who had carried out the bloody massacre in the south of France had within hours gotten to this address in London. But how? It wouldn't be too difficult. They could have driven their Citroens to a nearby small private airport and, like Hijaz, have gotten into another twin-engined Cessna for Heathrow Airport. Then they would expect, without ever having to go through Customs and Immigration formalities, to join Hijaz in the Boeing, taxiing on the runway. So they'd arrived at Heathrow and found the Boeing wasn't available. There was no reason why they shouldn't then pass through Customs and Immigration in the usual way. There were no descriptions available and no alert out for the Beaulieu killers in England.

Regan studied the facade of the house for the last time. It was probably in this house that the pro-Arab group had planned the massacre. Over a dozen gendarmes and Israelis had died and it still hadn't stopped the atom power deal between the Arabs and the French. But all Regan could really think of was the wounded policeman, and something closer to him, the dead Jo. And how Hijaz must pay.

Outside the house Regan met Harris, who told him that

Maynon and Haskins were parked in Maynon's car in Broadley Street, a hundred yards north of the square. Regan walked across the square and north up to Broadley Street. He knew why the senior cops were parked there. They were deliberately giving Regan the free run of the square, deliberately steering clear.

Maynon's driver got out of the car, and Regan sat in behind the steering wheel.

"Hello, Jack." The superintendent made his curt greeting, no expression in his voice.

Haskins's greeting was even more abrupt, a nod.

"How's it going?"

"Nothing I can't handle."

"I know that."

Regan told them of his positive identification of one of the Beaulieu killers, and that he felt the wounded policeman was in a serious condition.

"What have you worked out?" Maynon asked gently.

"Specifics?" Regan hadn't formed a detailed plan. He told them that.

"Why did you cut off their electricity?"

"They may have television in the apartment. The BBC's arrived. Before ITV for once. I don't want Hijaz and company getting information from a TV set, or being made overly nervous by seeing TV shots of crowds and cops."

"We're going to have a traffic problem if this doesn't sort itself out," Haskins said.

"Who cares about traffic?" Regan said. "Traffic doesn't matter. These men aren't going anywhere."

157

"When will you have a plan, Jack?" Maynon asked.

"Initially I suggest we follow the conclusions we all made after the Balcombe Street siege. A cooling-off period, then we try dialogue. But first a few hours while we all relax, get our bearings, get phones installed, communications sorted out, lay of country studied, then we'll make the decision of how long to wait, or whether to flush them out."

Maynon was studying the house, nodding slowly. "Okay," he said, like it was a detailed plan and had received his imprimatur. "Remember one key thing. The public's looking on. We're standing out like a newly whitewashed toilet wall. Don't give 'em a chance to write graffiti."

Regan stayed with them another five minutes. He wanted to reassure them that he was not about to embark on any crazy or injurious course of action. Of course from now on Maynon would be tuned in by walkie-talkie to every word exchanged by every copper in the square. Nonetheless Regan had to give the verbal assurances that he wouldn't be doing any rough riding. That's what he said, and they seemed to be assured. They didn't seem to realize that he was lying.

He left the car but he wasn't happy. He didn't trust Maynon, not an inch, nor Haskins. The second it suited them, they'd get him relieved as officer in charge. Meanwhile he could stand about and carry the can if it went wrong. Then he realized that they were right not to trust him. Implicit in any course of action he was currently planning was that he was about to betray the whole of the Met's trust in him.

He walked along the southeast corner of the square. Armed cops were still arriving and sprinting all over the shop, like this was a preparation for a Normandy landing. He met Harris and told him to organize a canteen lorry. Harris had anticipated him. One had already arrived, and another one was on the way.

"You can go off for an hour," he said to Harris. "I may have to take a break later. I really will have to shave for the TV cameras. You take an hour and be back at one."

Harris was looking at his watch. "What time d'you think it is? It's eleven o'clock, not twelve," he told Regan.

"Right." Regan adjusted his watch. "I've just come from France. They're an hour ahead."

"I thought we're all on Greenwich mean time now."

"No," Regan said. "The frogs are an hour ahead of us now."

Harris went off. Regan sought out the canteen van, but he was not really interested in much more than a cup of coffee while he tried to think the whole thing through. He was officer in charge, and basically that meant he had to come up with an initiative in the next few hours, or at the latest by evening, or gradually the media would overtake the situation, build it up into a major crisis. Then the general public and its TV interviewers would only be satisfied by the presence and statements of the big guns. If the siege wasn't over by nightfall, the commissioner would have to show up at the scene and give interviews. If it wasn't over by tomorrow morning, then the usual queue of parrots in the House of Commons would be putting down questions. This was time suspended, in no-man's-land. Regan knew his superiors were deliber ately standing back to give him room, were sitting it out while he drank his free coffee and worked out some trick to get four guys and at least one gun out of that house.

Meanwhile a cop was in a serious condition. Regan, as soon as he'd arrived at the scene, had immediately given permission for several press photographers to approach the stretcher and get the big Nikon close-ups. Those photographs would be in every evening paper. Those pictures would get the public firmly on the side of law and order and any police initiative, even if it went wrong. From the political point of view, it was almost worth sitting it out for a few hours till the first newspapers hit the street. The fact was, Regan couldn't see the incident ending without bloodshed.

He finished his coffee, walked over to the mobile communications center, and made four phone calls. The first was to St. George's Hospital, to check the condition of the shot constable. He was still in a critical condition, but there had been a mild improvement. The second call was the Bahrain embassy. He talked to a first secretary—he stated his business. Was there anyone available, perhaps the ambassador, or a senior official, who would be prepared to come to North Square, Bayswater, to talk to a Mr. Hijaz holed up in a house? Obviously the news of the siege in North Square had leaked through to the embassy. In a few economical, curt, and stiff-lipped sentences, he was told that the incident at North Square was of no interest to the ambassador, who would not be intervening.

Regan decided to talk to Maynon again. The man was in his office at the Yard.

"I've just one question," he stated. "D'you think the top brass are looking for anything like the scenario on the recent Balcombe Street siege, or the Spaghetti House siege? I'm wondering why I'm being given room."

"Don't quote me on this. The Spaghetti House and the Balcombe Street sieges were PR jobs for police recruitment. This is different. This is political. This involves the Arabs, whom this country has to be friendly to. At the same time this man has shot a policeman. Justice must be done. Also the embassy here has written him off. Up to the moment all the public knows is that this is an incident involving one man and three confreres who've wounded a policeman in Bayswater. They don't know about Beaulieu. We want the scenario kept small, at your level."

He phoned Detective Sergeant Carter, his usual assistant, pal, oracle of reasonable advice freely given and spiced always with the right blend of slyness, cynicism, and Yard politics. "George, meet me now, the canteen lorry in North Square."

Carter arrived twenty minutes later. Regan had already gotten him a coffee. Carter grimaced as he tasted it, but he drank it.

"What d'you think, George?"

Carter shrugged.

"You know the whole story?"

"Yeah, I got it all—the raid on the south of France nick, the private plane at Heathrow Airport—from Haskins."

"What d'you think?"

Carter hesitated, then shrugged. "Let me give you an honest and dishonest opinion, guv. I put it that way because I can't prove this opinion. But I think you're being set up."

Regan was studying the young man's face intently.

"I think you've been set up right from the beginning. From the moment the ACC and the Special Branch dumped you in it. You've gone from one laundry to another doing other people's washing. Now you're here in a political siege in London West Two, and there's no way any OC is going to come out of it with high marks. You'll come out dead or disgraced, but no way the Golden Boy. How am I doing so far?" Carter asked gently.

"Go on," Regan told him.

"I'd say they cast you in the mug's role right from the beginning."

"Is that right?" No annoyance in Regan's voice as he assimilated Carter's words, but wasn't quite sure if they were on beam. "I was set up at the beginning. But surely that ended when I solved the whereabouts of Haffasa's killer. Once I'd phoned from La Reserve to Maynon I was put in the picture. From that point I don't think I was a patsy anymore."

"You were. You are," Carter said flatly. "No OC on this North Square siege is going to come out a hero. I heard you more or less blackmailed Maynon. You wouldn't give over the bloke's address in the south of France till you got the full story. Pulling a stunt like that on Maynon doesn't make you his most popular cop. He's delighted to make you OC, to pay you back, 'cos you're going to fuck your-self, guv. . . ."

Suddenly Regan knew Carter was right. Carter was telling the simple truth and he hadn't seen it. He'd had all the letters but he hadn't spelled it out. Slowly the anger began to well up in him. Anger at himself, anger at his bosses, fury at Hijaz, the man who had killed Jo and was now set up to wreck his career. Nobody in charge was about to get out of the North Square siege clear, commended, with a career still intact—a lunatic Bahraini, three professional killers, and a gun. No way that lot could be sorted out without one final, hellish incident.

He'd had a half-formed plan since he'd talked to Harris at what he thought was twelve o'clock, but was actually eleven. The plan worked with the coincidence of his getting the London Electricity Board to the siege house to switch off electricity. For the plan to work, the four men in the house must not watch television or have any other contact with the outside world. The phone too had been cut off, or at least rerouted through the exchange for an intercept at the mobile communications van.

At three-thirty Regan left the police canteen lorry. Everything had fallen into place in his mind. All he'd wanted was the attitudes, the reasonings, sorted out. If he died, he didn't want those last seconds spent with the added agony of knowing he'd been suckered himself. He'd have to know that he'd taken the initiative and reworked a set of reasons so that they were sound for him. "George, I appreciated the advice. Thanks," said Regan.

Carter nodded and walked off.

Regan made one last telephone call. It was to the armorer at Scotland Yard, instructing him to come out to North Square with a quality rifle and ammunition, and a docket to be made out to Regan which he would sign.

At four o'clock, he toured the square with Harris and a couple of DI's from Bayswater. He was pleased to find the atmosphere among the cops relaxed, the tension reduced to very low key. The square, the mews behind the south side, was now evacuated and blocked off. The police staffing had been reduced to eighty as soon as police sharpshooters had been installed in selected aeries overlooking all exits, doors, and windows of the Hijaz house. The public had dwindled to a hundred and fifty of the staunchly curious, still lingering, though excluded from all views of the house. There were a dozen disconcerted pressmen wandering around—nobody could give them any more information than that an Arab had shot a cop and was holed up with some pals in a converted house. Regan returned to the communications van. He and his colleagues would wait it out until dark.

Maynon phoned at 6:30 P.M. He wanted to know how it was going. Regan told him—everything under control. Regan said he had no initiative planned for at least another five or six hours.

At seven o'clock a truck arrived from the Central Electricity Generating Board, and a couple of electricians unloaded six halogen floodlights and started to set them up on the front, side, and rear of the Hijaz building. Regan told the sparks to get it right. There would be no testing. He would shout at some point for the lights to come on, and they'd better come on.

At seven-thirty Regan picked up the phone which had been rerouted through the mobile communications van and dialed the number of Hijaz's apartment.

He sat and waited for ten minutes. He could imagine the atmosphere in the darkened apartment as the four men listened to the ringing phone.

Suddenly the phone was picked up.

"Hijaz? Regan." There was a pause. "Hijaz. You there?"

The voice came back, more a growl than a word. "Yes."

"We're not going to piss around with you or your pals. We're coming in to get you at nine o'clock exactly. That's the deal. Unless you walk out of the house, and you'll walk out the front door with that gun of yours and then throw it out into the street, not a minute before nine o'clock, not a second after, I'm coming in. That's all I have to say. Nine o'clock."

Regan replaced the phone and turned to Harris and the other two DI's sitting on the bench inside the mobile communications van. They'd heard everything he'd said. If he lived, and there was an inquiry afterward, they would be the witnesses to his apparent innocence, the lie to his cold-blooded guilt. He then dialed Maynon's extension at the Yard. He got through to a secretary, left the message of what he'd said to Hijaz, and added that he'd appreciate it if Maynon could be at North Square by eight-thirty at the latest. Five minutes later Maynon called the mobile communications van. He'd received the message. He would be there at eight-thirty.

Regan now took the rifle he'd obtained from the Yard armorer out of its canvas bag. It was a .404 sharpshooter Remington, with a 4X Bushnell telescopic sight. It was not a very sophisticated rifle, but a reliable one. He checked the gun, snapped a first bullet into the breech. He turned to Harris and asked the inspector whether he would accompany him on a last tour of the square. Harris nodded.

They set off across the enclosed silence of the night square, small movements of cops in the shadows, flashlights clicking on and off, all the houses now evacuated, not one watt of light from any window. Streetlamps were burning on three sides of the square. But the south side, a chimera of shapes of various intensities of darkness, a stillness there like a twig had cracked under a predator's foot in a night jungle. The silence pregnant, waiting for something to happen to measure its potential.

Regan and Harris proceeded with caution, heads down, striding fast. They looked in the shadows for the men who were guarding them. Any of those men could bear a vital function in an hour from now. They looked for the silhouettes against the roof profiles of four buildings. Up there, with identical Remingtons, four highly trained sharpshooters. Two would have the new Rank UV nightsights. They looked for faults in the composition of the spider's web of security that covered all exits from the square. There was no way out now for Hijaz and the other three. But they would not learn that. Regan had left an absolute order with the inspector running the mobile communications van. He must intercept, but not answer, any outgoing call from the Hijaz apartment. They had made their beds; now they must lie and sweat in them.

Regan timed his arrival at the east side of the square for about a minute to eight. He had just talked again to the two electricians who had rigged the half dozen floodlights when he saw a movement from the Hijaz house. Somewhere in the facade of darkness fifty yards away a door had opened. Regan howled one word and ran. "Lights!"

One of the electricians was so alarmed by the frantic shout that he fumbled the switch gear he was carrying. There was a four seconds' delay punctuated with the man's curses, then the south end of the square lit up like it had been hit by napalm.

The four men were trapped, frozen, blinded by light, a tableau like a child's game of pretending to be statues. Hijaz, armed with a submachine gun, the others unarmed. Regan was running at full tilt at them, was twenty feet away from Hijaz, when the blinded man swung the M-38 and fired. Regan felt the physical pulse of bullets pass within inches to the left and right of his temples as he threw himself in a bone-jarring crunch forward onto the pavement.

But in the fall he fired twice. The first bullet blew off Hijaz's right ear and some of his head in a bag of blood. The second went through his chest, killed him as he stood there, rocked him as he made a first dead step sideways in flight. Hijaz went down. Six hands shot up above the heads of his three colleagues. The movement seemed interlinked, a natural reflex, but there was nothing natural about the white faces and the man soaking in a floodlit pool of blood on the pavement. And Regan was still lying on the pavement, gunsight pressed to his eyes, willing them, praying that one of them would make a move to grab for the fallen M-38. More must die for Jo and the others in Beaulieu. But the three wouldn't move; they robbed him of the chance for total revenge.

Two and a half hours later Regan entered Maynon's office. Maynon's eyes were cold fury. He made a sharp brushing gesture toward a seat.

Regan sat down.

Maynon was reading a file. Regan could identify it. He'd seen it on several occasions over the years. It was his file. Why, Regan wondered, was Maynon reading his file? He cautioned himself to silence. Maynon's eyes would not come off the pages. But Regan guessed he was not reading them. Maynon was about to say something and was phrasing it internally first, and refining it.

Then he looked up. "You murdered him." Maynon said it so quietly that Regan for a second thought he was over his fury. He wasn't. "I'm staggered. You murdered him in cold blood." This said much louder.

"I deny that, sir." Regan's voice was low.

"The watch on Hijaz's hand was reading one hour fast. The watches on his companions all read one hour fast. They're on French time. You knew that. When you arrived in London, your watch was one hour fast. So you ordered them to come out of the house at 9:00 P.M. You knew perfectly well they'd come out an hour earlier."

"There's always an announcement on the plane to correct watches forward," Regan countered.

"There isn't, Regan. Not on a private Cessna. Hijaz and the other three arrived on private Cessnas. In normal circumstances maybe they would have spotted the airport clocks. But in both cases on touchdown they had plenty on their minds. Hijaz was arrested; the other three had just come from a mass murder." Maynon seemed to be getting more furious. "The point is, it was no gamble. You had all the cards, it either worked or it wouldn't work, and if it didn't you'd think of some other way to murder them. I'm accusing you of murder. You pretended they were trying to sneak out of the house early. You used that as an excuse to open fire on that man."

"Ask a half dozen witnesses at the scene. Hijaz fired at me first," Regan said flatly.

"He fired because he saw a cop running flat out toward him with a rifle."

Regan said nothing. The silence in the office grew heavier.

Maynon's eyes were still boring into him. "I understand you were involved with the girl killed in the Beaulieu raid."

Regan said nothing.

Silence again, heavy on the air, and Maynon still working it out, the fury trying to form itself into decision. Regan was not helping him a bit.

"He killed your girl, or was instrumental in her death,

six gendarmes dead, a wounded London constable."

Regan said nothing.

Maynon made up his mind. "Get out of here. Get out of my sight for a week at least. Take a holiday. Spend seven days thinking about what you've done today, how you arrived at your decisions, why you decided you would be able to live with them. I think you should resign from the force. I think this time you went just too bloody far. . . ."

Regan stood up, walked to the door and out. He had no answer to any observations Maynon had made.

He took a day extra—went to Aldeburgh for six days, then on to Norwich for two. He was drunk every night from 6:00 P.M. until, with protests, the hotel barmen threw him out. He thought about what Maynon had said. It didn't make a fart's worth of difference. He could live with what he'd done. Sod them all, he'd live to be a hundred and he wouldn't lose one hour's sleep over it.